I0595096

Oliver Optic, American Popular Literature Collection

Switch Off
The war of the students

ISBN/EAN: 9783337390211

Printed in Europe, USA, Canada, Australia, Japan

Cover: Foto ©Andreas Hilbeck / pixelio.de

More available books at **www.hansebooks.com**

THE LAKE SHORE SERIES.

SWITCH OFF;

OR,

THE WAR OF THE STUDENTS.

BY

OLIVER OPTIC,

AUTHOR OF "YOUNG AMERICA ABROAD," "THE ARMY AND NAVY STORIES,"
"THE WOODVILLE STORIES," "THE BOAT-CLUB STORIES,"
"THE STARRY FLAG STORIES," ETC.

BOSTON:
LEE AND SHEPARD, PUBLISHERS.
NEW YORK:
LEE, SHEPARD AND DILLINGHAM.
1873.

ELECTROTYPED AT THE
BOSTON STEREOTYPE FOUNDRY,
No. 19 Spring Lane.

TO

MY YOUNG FRIEND

"DOWNSEY"

𝔗𝔥𝔦𝔰 𝔅𝔬𝔬𝔨

IS AFFECTIONATELY DEDICATED.

THE LAKE SHORE SERIES.

1. *THROUGH BY DAYLIGHT;* or, The Young Engineer of the Lake Shore Railroad.

2. *LIGHTNING EXPRESS;* or, The Rival Academies.

3. *ON TIME;* or, The Young Captain of the Ucayga Steamer.

4. *SWITCH OFF;* or, The War of the Students.

5. *BRAKE UP;* or, The Young Peacemakers. (*In press.*)

6. *BEAR AND FORBEAR;* or, The Young Skipper of Lake Ucayga.

PREFACE.

"Switch Off" is the fourth of The Lake Shore Series, and was one of the serials which appeared in Oliver Optic's Magazine. Its principal incidents relate to the students of the Toppleton Institute, among whom the war indicated on the title-page occurred. The story is told by one of the young men, who is a prominent actor in the events he narrates. Tommy Toppleton again appears, and is even more overbearing and tyrannical than before; but the reader will be willing to congratulate him, at the end, upon the happy influence of all his trials and troubles on his character, and, perhaps, be better prepared to believe that "oft from apparent ills our blessings rise."

It has been the purpose of the author in this volume still further to illustrate the precept of the gospel, "Love your enemies;" and the conduct of Ned towards his defeated and mortified enemy is earnestly recommended as a safe rule for life. The manner in which peace happened to be made between the rival Institutes has always been found to work quite as well in actual experience as in the story.

HARRISON SQUARE, MASS.,
August 24, 1869.

CONTENTS.

CONTENTS.

CHAPTER XIX.

CHAPTER XX.

CHAPTER XXI.

CHAPTER XXII.

CHAPTER XXIII.

CHAPTER XXIV.

CHAPTER XXV.

CHAPTER XXVI.

SWITCH OFF;

OR,

THE WAR OF THE STUDENTS.

CHAPTER I.

READY FOR A START.

"ORDER—arms!" said Major Tommy Toppleton, mounted on his sorrel pony, and facing the battalion formed of the students of the Toppleton Institute.

The buts of the light muskets clanged in unison on the gravel walk, where the column was drawn up. It was early on Monday morning, and the young soldiers were in excellent spirits—better than they were likely to be at a later hour in the day, for the programme included a fatiguing march. On the road leading from the Institute grounds stood three wagons, each drawn by two horses, upon which were loaded the baggage, provisions, and camp equipage of the battalion.

At the head of the column was the students' band of ten pieces, besides a drum corps of eight, and two fifers. Signor Perelli, our music teacher, had bestowed incredible care and pains upon these amateur musicians, and those who were competent judges declared that the result was highly creditable to his skill and perseverance. In other words, the band played very well, though it did not undertake to compete with Gilmore, Strauss, Jullien, or even with the Ucayga Cornet Band. The drum corps was a perfect success, for most of its members had been in practice over a year.

Not a few of the people of Middleport had gathered in front of the Institute to witness the parade, for the occasion was no ordinary one, and the programme of the battalion had been thoroughly discussed for weeks. In years before, the students had camped out during the June vacation. During the preceding season the Toppletonians had pitched their tents on the Horse Shoe, where the famous battles between the rival academies had taken place, as my friend Captain Wolf Penniman has related in his story.

Camping out had become rather stale with the students, and they longed for a new sensation. If they could have encamped on the Horse Shoe, and had another conflict with the Wimpletonians, perhaps it would have satisfied them. But there was no prospect of any sport of this kind, for Waddie Wimpleton, the haughty, untamed, and tyrannical, was as mild and gentle as a lamb. It was said among the fellows that he had experienced religion, or something of that sort. It was certain he was not the boy he used to be. He had voluntarily resigned his positions as president of the Steamboat Company and major of the battalion. Though Ben Pinkerton was commander of the forces on the other side of the lake, it was supposed that Waddie's influence as a peacemaker was sufficient to control the movements of the troops, and prevent them from engaging in another conflict with the fellows on our side of the lake.

Besides, there was another circumstance which seemed to interfere to keep the peace between the boys of the two Institutes. A military gentleman, residing at Ucayga, had become interested in the two battalions of juvenile soldiers, and had offered a prize of a magnificent standard to the one which should excel the other in company and battalion drill. With the vanity natural to boys, each party believed that all the skill and precision was upon its own side, and both had accepted the invitation to drill for the banner. This great event was to come off on the following Friday morning, at Centreport. The place had been fixed by lot; and, when the arrangement had been completed, it suggested the present movement of our battalion.

The Toppletonians did not care to encamp at any point near enough to Centreport to enable them to keep their engagement, and when Captain Briscoe jocosely proposed that the little army should march round to the other side of the lake by the way of Hitaca, the idea was received with tremendous enthusiasm. The excursion would be a tour of camp duty, with an ever-changing scene, and with no lack of novelty and excitement. We voted, almost unanimously, that the long tramp of seventy miles was just the thing we wanted.

It would afford us opportunity to display our new uniforms, our band and drum corps, our drill and marching, to people on the route who had hardly ever seen a company of soldiers. We should astonish the Hitacaites with our music and parade, excite the admiration of the ladies in general, and the young ladies in particular, and make us all first-class lions. The people would turn out to behold us, bestow delicate attentions upon us, and entertain us with generous hospitality. We had all the elements for a splendid parade, including our stylish uniforms, good music, and well-trained companies.

For two weeks hardly anything was talked about but this tour of camp duty. Those who received the plan coldly at first, soon became enthusiastic. Those who growled at the idea of marching twenty miles in a day were persuaded to believe that our progress would be a continued triumph, and that it would be accomplished in six or seven hours, so that there would be plenty of time to rest. The authorities of the Institute objected to the plan, but as Major Tommy Toppleton favored it, there was not much to be said against it. His father was compelled to indorse the march; and, of course, the instructors were obliged to withdraw all opposition.

Two of the teachers, besides the drill-master, were detailed to accompany the battalion in carriages, and prevent it from robbing hen-roosts, or capturing any of the towns on the route. But when Tommy heard of this little arrangement he was as indignant as though the professors had given him a thrashing, and interposed his veto. He would not have any school-masters dogging his steps, and spying into his actions. He hated spies. The battalion was composed of young gentlemen, and if they were a little fast at times, they knew how to behave themselves, and did not need any pedagogues to watch them. He could take care of his force himself. So the instructors were permitted to spend their vacation in pursuits more congenial to their tastes than following a multitude of crazy boys, under a crazy leader. Perhaps it would have been better for Tommy if he had permitted these guardians of the peace to attend the battalion.

We were all ready to start. The baggage wagons were to fall in behind the column, and the drivers were on their boxes. Everybody was in high spirits, and anticipated the greatest time known in the annals of the Toppleton Institute. Major Tommy, in particular, was in full feather; for he was the commander of the expedition, and a march of a week through places which suggested honors and ovations was an event which was calculated to stimulate his bump of self-esteem.

On the preceding Saturday, the stockholders of the Lake Shore Railroad had held their annual meeting. On the year before, the present president had actually been defeated on the first ballot, and "your humble servant" elected in his place. Not caring to endure the constant browbeating and annoyance to which I should have been subjected had I taken the office, and because I really believed then that Tommy ought to have it, I had declined. Then, by a tremendous effort on the part of the president's friends, and particularly on the part of Wolf Penniman, who pleaded for him as though he had been a friend in distress, Tommy received a bare majority of the votes cast.

I was sorry afterwards that I refused the position; for Tommy, always overbearing and tyrannical, became so to such an extent that the fellows had been on the verge of mutiny for a year. They had waited with impatience for the return of the annual elections, intending to pitch him down from his high positions. But Tommy and his father had provided for this emergency. The former had always nominally held — as, in fact, the rest of the students owned their stock — a large proportion of the shares. If a boy left the Institute during the year, his stock was made over to Tommy, or to some of his toadies, for he had a small army of satellites of this species. The result was, that the president was reëlected by a small majority. Feeling that he was secure in his high position, he had taken no pains to conciliate those who condemned his tyranny, and, if possible, he was more unpopular than ever.

The students had become pretty thoroughly disgusted with the management of the Lake Shore Railroad. Although the business of the company was still carried on in their name; though the stock was bought, sold, and transferred on the books; though the boys discharged the duties of their several offices, — they had but little interest in the corporation. They had no real power. If the superintendent, the road-master, or the directors did anything, it was by order of Tommy or his father. But, I ought to add, in justice to Major Toppleton, that there was not a student in the Institute, who had been there a year, that did not know all about the details of running a railroad, who was not familiar with stock operations, and who was not prepared to discharge his duty as an official in a railroad company. As a means of instruction, it was still a good thing; but it had ceased to be a source of amusement, as it would have been if the president had not ruled so arbitrarily.

As the railroad president, Tommy was safe for another year. Though dissatisfied, our fellows had already begun to gather up the stock by helping out weaker ones in their lessons, or by the purchase of it with money, peanuts, and cream-cakes. The election of a commanding officer of the battalion usually came off on the same day as the railroad meeting; but it had been postponed to the following Tuesday, by what influence I do not know. Those who accomplished this purpose either forgot that on this day we should be on the march, or they expected to derive some advantage from the fact.

Tommy Toppleton declared that he was sure of being elected; and I think he was sincere in his belief. He had many devoted adherents, who bowed down to his power and influence; but there were just as many active opponents, and a great middle class who were not partisans either for or against him. Electioneering on both sides was carried on with spirit and energy, and the contest promised to be an exciting one.

CHAPTER II.

ON THE MARCH.

THE battalion stood at "order arms," waiting for the next movement. Major Tommy galloped his sorrel charger up and down the line, looking with great solemnity at the troops. We in the line wondered what was going to happen, though we were all sufficiently aware of Tommy's propensity for making speeches to suspect that he meditated a flight of rhetoric on the present occasion. The opportunity seemed to be too good for him to neglect. He would not have thought of making a speech to the battalion alone; but the instructors and quite a respectable crowd of the town's people were present, and we knew the oration was intended for them rather than for us, to whom it was addressed.

"Soldiers," Tommy began, with a flourish of his sword,—a very elegant toy, which added much vim to his words, — "we are about to commence a long march."

"What's the use of saying that? We knew it before," said, in a low tone, the first lieutenant of Company B, who stood near me.

"We are going without any of our instructors, entirely upon our own responsibility."

"We know that too," growled the lieutenant; and no one will suspect that he was a partisan of the major.

"Soldiers, we must remember the uniform that we wear, and never disgrace it. We must bear in mind that we are the soldiers of the Toppleton Institute, upon which rests no stain of disgrace or dishonor. Wherever we go, let it be our purpose to reflect credit and honor upon the institution. We claim to be young gentlemen; let us conduct ourselves as such, whether we be in the halls of the Institute, or amid the solitudes of nature."

"He stole that," hummed the discontented lieutenant of Company B.

"Soldiers, we are a military organization, subject to the rules of military discipline. The first duty of a soldier is to obey the orders of his superiors. I expect from you, during the march that is before us, the most implicit obedience to your officers. If any one, officer or private, behaves himself in an unsoldierly manner, he shall be promptly tried by court martial, and punished for his offence."

"Court martial!" exclaimed the grumbler of Company B. "If Tommy Toppleton don't conduct himself according to his buncombe standard, I go for trying him by court martial."

Tommy's allusion to military discipline looked as though he had obtained a new idea. A court martial was a thing unknown in the experience of our little army. Tommy had threatened the thing once or twice when the boys were crooked, though delinquents were reported to the principal of the Institute, and punished by him. But it was a fact that the major had been studying up courts martial; and when he mentioned the matter, we were satisfied that he would be on the lookout for some one to court martial. It was evident that he wished to go through with the ceremony of a military court, and we saw that it would be well for us to be prudent, or he would soon find a victim.

Tommy proceeded to explain the order of march, the rules of the camp and bivouac, and repeated his injunctions that all the members of the battalion should behave with perfect propriety, the latter of which could only be meant in a Pickwickian sense, and was uttered to produce a proper impression upon the instructors and other outsiders.

"Shoulder — arms!" shouted he, when he had finished his oration.

We shouldered, broke into sections, and moved off. The baggage wagons fell in behind, and the long tramp was actually commenced. The band played "The Girl I left behind me," which, however, had no special significance on the present occasion, inasmuch as we were all too young to have sweethearts. Major Tommy rode in solemn majesty at the head of the column, the boys and girls in the streets gazing at him in wonder and admiration. The sorrel pony, as well as the rider, seemed to "feel his oats," prancing and curvetting in a very impressive manner.

In less than half an hour we had passed the last house in the town. Thus far we had marched with the utmost precision, and the band had played nearly all the time, relieved at intervals by the drum corps. Of course we all expected to make a show when we passed any houses, or there were any people to see us; but we did not like to be kept in the strait jacket of precision when there was no occasion for a sensation, and when there was nothing but the squirrels and the robins to be moved by a martial display. We expected the order for the "route step," which permitted us to march in a free and easy manner. It did not come, and the band and the drum corps blowed and pounded just as though we had been in the midst of a populous city.

"Tommy is ugly to-day," said the lieutenant of Company B. "He means to make us work our passage."

"I am afraid he is," I replied. "But it is not very uncommon for him."

"I should think he would remember that to-morrow will be election day. What's the use of tooting so out here!" added the malcontent, alluding to the music of the band.

"No use; but it's Tommy's will."

"No talking in the ranks there!" exclaimed Tommy, who had halted his steed at the side of the road to survey his command. "Captain Skotchley, you will keep in your proper position."

I obeyed the order; but, as Tommy rode forward, I ventured to suggest that the route step would be agreeable to the privates.

"You will mind your own business, Captain Skotchley, and remember that I command the battalion. I don't need any advice," was the ungracious reply.

By regular promotions I had become the captain of Company B. My advancement was not due to Tommy's favor, for I was not one of his toadies. I had taken no part in the battles on the Horse Shoe the year before, when the conduct of the little major had been so overbearing that I could not endure it. I was charged with being a deserter. I wrote to my father, asking him to take me away from the Institute; but he was an old friend of Major Toppleton, senior, and a peace was patched up between us. I was restored to my rank; but Tommy hated me as he did the evil one, because I would not toady to him.

Why should I? My father was not less wealthy than his. Our social position was just as good. I always made it a point to be a gentleman. I had my friends among the poor as well as the rich; and I don't think I ever put on airs. I always had a profound respect and admiration for Wolf Penniman, and we were the very best of friends. He always called me the "dignified student," though I don't think there was any particular reason for doing so, unless it was that I was too dignified to be trodden beneath the feet of Tommy Toppleton. I always liked a good time, and went in for one when there was a chance.

Without egotism I may say that I stood well with the fellows in the Institute — that is, with all those whose good opinion was worth having. I base my judgment of this feeling upon the fact that they elected me the president of the railroad company over Tommy Toppleton, the year before, and had given me almost a majority the present year. More than this, in the counsels of the opposition, I had been invited to stand as a candidate for major, at the coming election. Briscoe ranked me, and was a very good fellow, though a little disposed to be hot-headed at times. I refused to stand in his way, believing him justly entitled to the office if Tommy was defeated, as the opposition hoped and expected he would be on the following day. Some of the fellows told the captain of Company A that I had declined in his favor, and I did not lose anything in his estimation by the act.

Tommy did not give us the route step, and we concluded he intended to worry and fatigue us as much as he could; but we were too good soldiers to disobey orders, at least at this stage of the march. We advanced with as much precision as though the eyes of admiring thousands had been fixed upon us. We were ascending the gentle undulation of a long hill, about four miles from Middleton, when we saw a young man in a wagon, with a very pretty girl at his side, driving a spirited horse. The band was laboriously wailing out the solemn strains of "Hail, Columbia," for it had about exhausted its *repertoire* of pieces; and the bass drummer pounded out his part as though he knew not the meaning of weariness. The horse attached to the wagon, which appeared to be a four-year-old colt, began to snort, and exhibit an evident disinclination to "face the music."

Pretty girl was alarmed, as well she might be, for the capricious animal reared and plunged in a fearful manner. The young man holding the reins was master of the situation, though he appeared to have his hands full.

Major Tommy was riding on the flank of the battalion, as the head of the column approached the furious horse. He dashed forward with a flourish, when the leader of the band, seeing that the music frightened the colt, and not wishing to be responsible for a catastrophe, had silenced the players.

"Why don't you play? What did you stop for?" shouted the major, angrily. "Strike up again!"

The leader tooted with his bugle, and the bass drummer hammered out the initial notes of the piece. The terrified animal, which had begun to take a reasonable view of the situation, reared and plunged again. Pretty girl screamed, as pretty girls do when they are alarmed, and the colt was frightened all the more.

"I say, cap'n, just stop the music for half a minute — won't you, if you please?" said the driver, appealing to Tommy, who had now resumed his place at the head of the battalion.

"No, sir! I won't stop the music," replied Tommy, rudely; and he appeared to enjoy the terror of the pretty girl, and the antics of the horse.

"Only half a minute! Clarissa is scared half to death," added the young man.

"Play away!" was the only reply the magnificent major deigned to make.

The colt stopped, stood up straight, and positively refused to advance another step. Then, as the band advanced, he began to back, until he had placed the wagon square across the road, between the major and the musicians.

"Stop the music," said Captain Briscoe, in a low tone.

The band ceased playing. Indeed, they could not well do otherwise, for the fractious colt, as the driver attempted to urge him forward, broke in upon their ranks, and then backed them out of the road, and out of their propriety at the same instant.

CHAPTER III.

MAJOR TOMMY UNHORSED.

"WHAT do you stop playing for?" demanded Major Tommy, furiously.

It was a stupid question, after the musicians had been driven out of the road by the antics of the colt. The head of the column had also been broken; for, though the Toppleton warriors were brave fellows, they did not like the idea of being ground under the wheels of the countryman's wagon, and they were prepared to make a safe retreat, without much regard to the order of their going. The major —as the colt finally stopped and stood impatiently pawing the ground — rode back to the spot where the head of the column ought to have been.

"You are a set of blockheads!" roared Tommy. "Are you afraid of a horse? Form in column! Play away, again."

"I say, cap'n, just hold on half a minute — won't you, till I get by?" called the driver of the unbroken colt.

"No, I won't."

"Don't be mean about it," added the countryman, rather angrily.

"Get out of the road!" cried Tommy.

"See here, you little cock-turkey: if you don't behave yourself, I'll snake you off that horse quicker than you can shut your eyes when it lightens!"

"Don't! Don't! I'm scart almost to death," gasped pretty girl. "Let me get out! We shall be killed."

And suiting the action to the words, pretty girl, as nimbly as a bird, jumped out of the wagon, and retreated from the scene of danger.

My company was still in good order, with the lieutenants in position in front of the platoons. I walked forward in season to hear Briscoe advise the leader of the band not to play. My judgment was, that Tommy was crazy to insist upon scaring the horse, when the danger was so great; and I was willing to back up the senior captain.

"Why don't you play, when I tell you to do so?" roared Tommy, furious at the disobedience of the band.

They did not say anything, but they did not blow. The colt, no longer hearing the music, and finding the road comparatively clear before 'him, allowed himself to be appeased by his driver. He stood tossing his head and pawing the ground; but he appeared to be conscious that he had won the battle, and to be entirely satisfied with himself. The young man in charge of him, doubtless thinking that discretion was the better part of valor, or that the battle was not worth fighting after the retreat of Clarissa, got out of the wagon, and took the colt by the bridle. Leading him out of the road, he patted his neck.

"Cap'n, your the meanest pup I've met since I was born," added the young man, when he had reduced the colt to a tolerably quiet state.

"None of your impudence, you rascal," replied Tommy.

"If I hadn't my hands full, I'd give you something besides impudence, you little snipper-snapper of a cock-turkey!"

"Form your company, Captain Briscoe!" growled Tommy.

The senior captain obeyed the command, and the battalion was again in marching order, with the scattered musicians reorganized at its head.

"Music!" shouted the commander. "Forward — march!"

The leader of the band was not one of Tommy's toadies, and, fortified by the senior captain's advice, he failed to give the key-note which was the signal for the musicians to play. The column began to move; but not a demi-semiquaver came from the band, — only the tap of the drummer.

"Halt!" cried the major, before the battalion had taken three steps. "Why don't you play?"

"I'm not going to scare that horse any more," replied the leader.

"You are not!" foamed Tommy, red with rage, as he pushed his horse up to the musician, and struck him over the shoulder with his sword.

"No, I'm not! I don't want to kill anybody."

It was evident that a victim for the court martial had been found; but it was certain that, if Fryes, the leader of the band, was "broken," we could have no more music, for the players could do nothing without him. He was the son of a German distinguished in musical circles, and inherited his skill from his father. He was a splendid fellow, and would have been an officer if he could have been spared from the band, so that his present service really involved a great sacrifice on his part.

"If you don't play, I'll march the battalion back to Middleport, and have you punished as you deserve," added Tommy.

We were not a little astonished that Fryes did not resent the indignity of the blow he had received, especially as he was a high-spirited fellow. I saw the leader glance at Briscoe, who nodded his head. Perhaps the senior captain was afraid that the irate major would march us back to the Institute, and thus defeat a little plan we had formed to remedy our grievances. Fryes understood the signal of Briscoe, and gave the key-note. The musicians were all ready.

"Forward — march!" shouted Tommy.

The first beat of the bass drum, with the accompanying blast of the brass instruments, waked up the eolt again, and, in spite of all the efforts of the countryman, again he stood up upon his hind feet. He was even more desperate than before, and in his furious struggles shook off the man. The instant he had freed himself from the control of the strong arm, — which I think was done by the breaking of the bridle, — he whirled around in the twinkling of an eye, without regard to the wagon attached to him. Cutting so short lifted up the body of the vehiele, and drawing out the snipe-bill, detaehed it from the forward wheels.

The colt now had it all his own way. The driver sprang forward and attempted to eatch him; but the beast seemed to flash rather than move in the ordinary way, and dashed off at a furious run in the direction from whieh he had eome. Pretty girl, on the bank at the side of the road, screamed again, as the catastrophe was consummated. The musieians ceased playing, in the exeitement of the moment, and the battalion was thrown into disorder.

"There, do you see what you've done!" howled the countryman, doubling up his fist at Tommy, as the colt disappeared behind a hill in front of us.

"I didn't do it," replied Tommy; and I judged, from his tone, that even he was not a little startled by the consequences of his folly. "Why didn't you take care of your horse?"

"Get off that nag!" said the young man, rushing upon Tommy, and seizing the pony by the bridle.

"Let me alone! Don't touch my horse!"

Before we were aware of his purpose, the excited man had dragged Tommy from his steed, and pitched him into the dirt in the middle of the road. But it presently appeared that he was not intent upon avenging the insults of Tommy, for he mounted the pony, and, grinding his heels into the flanks of the little charger, forced him into a run. He dashed up the hill, and disappeared beyond its crest.

Briscoe and I rushed forward to the assistance of Tommy, who, however, picked himself up with a facility which indicated that he was not seriously injured. I took his sword from the ground, where it had fallen in the sudden onslaught of the major's agile foe, and handed it back to him.

"Are you hurt, major?" asked Briscoe.

"No, I believe not," replied Tommy, feeling of his

injured leg, and assuring himself that it had sustained no damage.

"Is your leg all right?"

"Yes; but I should like to get hold of that fellow," answered Tommy, who had sufficiently recovered from his astonishment to begin to be angry at the savage treatment he had received.

"I don't think you would make much if you did get hold of him," I ventured to remark.

"Why not?" demanded the discomfited major, who .did not appear to see the point of my observation.

"He is too heavy for you."

"Do you think I will stand such usage as that?"

"I don't exactly see how you can help yourself, now that it is all over."

"I'll teach that fellow who I am."

"It seems to me that you will have to catch him before you teach him anything."

"The rascal has stolen my horse!"

"I don't think he meant to steal him," suggested Captain Briscoe. "He has only gone to find his own horse."

"He stole him, anyhow; and it will cost him a

penny for knocking me off in that style," continued Tommy, shaking his head, as the extent of his defeat seemed to crowd upon him. "That fellow don't know who I am."

"Perhaps he don't," I replied; and I couldn't help winking at Briscoe, though I am opposed to winking in any other than the natural way, in theory, if not in practice.

"What shall we do, Major Toppleton?" asked the senior captain, when Tommy had informed us what he intended to do, if he caught the countryman.

"Well, I don't know. I'm not going on this tramp without any horse."

"You will get your pony again," major, suggested Captain Briscoe.

"I want that man taken up and punished as he ought to be for knocking me off, and for taking my horse," added Tommy, savagely. "Why didn't you pitch into him, some of you, when he came at me?"

Neither of us ventured to make any reply to this reproachful question, for our sympathies were certainly with the young man — at least up to the point when he pulled Tommy off his horse.

"I don't think you had the pluck of a mosquito, or you would have punched him with your swords."

"Why didn't you do it yourself? You were nearer to him than we were," I replied.

"He didn't give me time."

"He didn't give us time, either."

"I didn't know what he was going to do till he had done it."

"Neither did we."

"No matter for that now; when we catch him we will give him fits. If the whole battalion can't handle that man, I think we had better take lessons in fighting. I'm going to capture him, and give him a thrashing for his impudence, if we see him again."

Briscoe looked at me with a meaning smile. We were not disposed to quarrel with our superior officer; but both of us believed the countryman had served him just right. It was a simple thing to stop the music for a few moments; but Tommy's stupid obstinacy always made him grossly unreasonable.

CHAPTER IV.

THE BATTLE AT THE FARM-HOUSE.

THE female companion of the countryman had already left the spot, and was hastening up the hill, probably very anxious to ascertain the fate of the colt. Major Tommy had made up his mind to do something desperate. He intended to find his assailant, and then charge upon him with the whole battalion; at any rate this was the interpretation which we gave to his words, looks, and gestures. If he ever fancied that he was insulted, or if he ever got the worst of it in any encounter in which he was himself the aggressor, he was not satisfied till he had obtained full satisfaction.

He was spiteful and revengeful. Because, during the military campaign of the preceding year, Wolf had gently declined to obey an order which involved the danger of killing or drowning a portion of the

Wimpletonians, he had followed him up with his spite until our friend was discharged from the employ of the Lake Shore Railroad. It was not in his nature, therefore, to permit his present assailant to escape without inflicting upon him the full penalty of his wrath.

Fryes, too, had incurred his displeasure by disobeying the major's unreasonable order. But Briscoe had counselled him to disregard this command; and our senior captain was not one who would disavow his act when the hour of reckoning came. He would stand by the leader of the band; and I intended to do so myself. The prospect, therefore, of a "jolly row" was very promising. I was only sorry that Briscoe had finally given the signal for Fryes to play, for this had caused all the real mischief. He told me he did so because the colt seemed to be quiet, and his driver held him by the head, so that he did not apprehend any more danger.

The battalion was in order in the road; and, after the major had sufficiently vented his indignation, he gave the command to march. The band played, and we ascended the hill. On the summit of it we obtained a view of the road for a mile. In the valley there was a farm-house, with a drive-way leading up to the barn in the rear. When we were near enough, we saw Tommy's pony fastened to the fence in front of the house. The colt, with the truck of the wagon, was in the yard. It was evident that this was the home of the countryman, and the fiery animal had sought the friendly shelter of the stable to save him from the terrors of the trumpet and bass drum. So far as we could judge, no injury had been done to man or beast.

When the head of the battalion arrived at the farm-house, the major gave the order to halt. His first movement was to mount his pony; and no opposition to this act was made by the occupants of the house. The man in charge of the colt detached him from the truck, and put him in the barn, probably to prevent him from being further demoralized by the martial array, and perhaps to enable him to meet the major on a better footing. While Tommy was mounting his horse, the man came out of the barn, and marched boldly up to the one hundred and twenty bayonets which our force presented.

"It's lucky for you that our colt wasn't hurt; if he had been, I would have taken it out of your hide," the countryman began, when he was within hailing distance of the major.

"What do you mean by knocking me off my horse?" responded Tommy.

"What do I mean? If you say much more, I'll duck you in that mud-hole over there. You could see that the music was scaring my colt; and I asked you, in a civil way, to stop it for half a minute, till I got by. If you hadn't been a hog, you would have done so," growled the rural gentleman.

"I'm not going to stop the music for every clown that comes along. You insulted me."

"Insulted you! I'm letting you off dog cheap! Now, go along about your business, before I'm tempted to put my claws upon you."

"Not yet," replied Tommy, shaking his head fiercely. "Do you know who I am?"

"I don't care who you are. If you were the Grand Mogul himself, I should speak my mind. I suppose you are that young pup of a Toppleton, that has it all his own way over to Middleport; but we don't train in that company, and when you come out here, you must behave yourself. I reckon you haven't any right to go tooting over our roads, and frightening horses with your racket. I'll let you off this time, as the colt isn't hurt, and nobody else isn't hurt."

"But I don't mean to let you off," retorted Tommy, irritated by this plain speech, and especially by the contempt manifested towards the house of Toppleton.

"O, don't you!" exclaimed the young man, with a broad grin.

"No, I don't. I'll pay you off for insulting me."

"Well, when you get ready, I want you to begin," chuckled the man. "But, if I have to take hold of you, I shall flop you over two or three times in that mud-hole, just enough to take the starch out of them fine clothes you wear."

"Get down on your knees and beg my pardon, and I will let you off," said Tommy, who evidently, after the expressive speech of the countryman, did not exactly relish the job he had undertaken.

"Well, that's a good one! Get down on my knees? I guess not! I never get down on my knees,

not even when I weed the onions. It wears out a
fellow's trousers. If you are not in a hurry, cap'n, I
wish you would wait just half a minute; I've got
some medicine in the barn that will just fit your
case."

This specimen of the high-spirited farmer rushed
into the barn, and presently returned with a cowhide
in one hand and a pitchfork in the other.

"If I'm going to stand up against the crowd, I
want this," he added, sticking the tines into the sod.
"If I'm going to deal with you alone, cap'n, I only
want this — and the mud-hole," he continued, flourishing the green hide. "You can go ahead any way
you like when you are ready, cap'n."

By this time, the "women folks" from the house,
including Clarissa, and an elderly man, who appeared
to be the father of the belligerent young man, had
assembled in the yard. The old gentleman had a
hoe in his hand, and had come forward to a point
within supporting distance of his son. He looked
like a Bunker Hill veteran, and regarded the threat-
ening conflict with imperturbable coolness. Probably he had already learned the merits of the case, for

he asked no questions, though he gave the major some sage advice, to the effect that he had done mischief enough, and had better go along about his business.

"Tom's a fool!" said Briscoe, impatiently, as we stood watching the issue of the controversy. "What does he mean to do?"

"I don't know," I replied; "but one stupid thing leads him into another."

But we were not left long in doubt in regard to what Tommy intended to do.

"Captain Skotchley!" called the major, in his imperative tone.

I walked up to him, and saluted with my sword.

"March your company to the rear of that rascal, and don't let him get away."

"I don't think he wants to get away," I replied.

"Then punch him with the bayonets, and we will take him in front. Make him a prisoner."

"Don't you do it, Ned," said Briscoe, in a low tone.

"I must respectfully decline to obey the order," I answered, firmly.

"You refuse?" gasped the major.

"I do."

"What do you mean?" howled Tommy, so mad that he could hardly help crying.

"Major Toppleton, I think you are all wrong in this business," I added. "We have no right to attack that man."

"Do you obey the orders of your commanding officer, or not?" demanded Tommy.

"I obey all reasonable orders," I replied.

"We will settle this with you another time," said the major, riding over to my company, whither I followed him.

I had given him another victim for the court martial, and I wondered what he would do next.

"Captain Skotehley is suspended from duty," continued the major. "He refuses to obey orders. Lieutenant Faxon will take command of the second company."

He repeated the order to the first lieutenant as he had given it to me.

"I must ask to be excused," replied Faxon.

"What! is there a mutiny in the battalion? Then Lieutenant Barnscott will command the company."

The second lieutenant had been bought up by the major, and was a willing tool. The privates had heard all these proceedings, and understood the merits of the question. When Barnscott undertook to march the company to the spot assigned to it, the majority refused to go.

"Mutiny!" shouted Tommy. "But I'll bring you to your senses!"

Twenty or twenty-five of the company followed Barnscott; the rest remained leaning on their guns in the road. Briscoe, when the order was given him to attack in front, followed my example; but his first lieutenant was one of the major's adherents, and obeyed the order with not more than thirty of his command. However, the attacking force was composed of about fifty, and Tommy was determined to be revenged.

The little major's military calculations were never very brilliant, and the old man and his son — the latter of whom seemed to regard the whole affair as a pleasant joke — obstinately refused to be flanked by Company B, and with the hoe and pitchfork kept the brave soldiers at bay. Tommy moved up himself with the first company, and ordered them to charge upon the young man and capture him. Before this could be done, however, the "women folks" appeared with a large tin wash-boiler, filled with hot water.

"Here, Jed!" called Clarissa, as she presented the young fellow with an immense syringe, used for showering plants with soap suds to destroy insects. "You can fix 'em in two minutes!"

Jed took the instrument, and filled it with water from the boiler, just as Company A charged bayonets, and began to move forward. Directing it at the advancing line, his ruddy face overspread with a jolly grin, he let fly the contents of the barrel. The old lady and Clarissa, with a couple of dippers, at the same time began to operate independently, dashing the hot water upon the column. The effect was decisive. The portions of the two companies engaged did not include the best fellows in the battalion, though, if they had, it is doubtful whether they could have stood up before a charge of hot water. The assailants broke, and retreated in disorder. The contents of Clarissa's tin cup, aimed at Tommy, drove him from the field, and he lost the battle.

The Battle at the Farm-House. Page 50.

CHAPTER V.

TO OBEY, OR NOT TO OBEY.

I THINK our brave fellows were more frightened than hurt; for, if the water in the wash-boiler was hot, it was not in condition to scald them after it had passed through the cold syringe. Some of them were a little red in spots on the face and hands; but, as warriors, in this piping time of peace, they had not been above dodging, and, in consequence, none of them were seriously damaged. Without using the obnoxious first line of the old couplet, they were in condition to fight another day.

The battle was certainly a very humorous one. Jed, in spite of his arduous labors, was convulsed with laughter. Clarissa, the pretty girl, was now very rosy, but whether from her exertions with the dipper or with laughing, I was unable to determine. The old farmer and his wife were both in excellent humor; and it was plain enough that we were to be laughed out of the battle, if we were not actually driven off the field. The mutinous troops who had refused to take part in the action were quite as much amused as the people of the farm.

Major Tommy Toppleton retreated before his routed column, which followed him down the road a short distance. The savage assailants did not offer to pursue their discomfited foe, and I had no doubt that the commander would call a council of war among his friends. I did not expect him to renew the attack under the present circumstances, or, at least, not till the water in the boiler had cooled off. Jed and his father, however, carried the kettle into the house, either to enable the old lady to continue her Monday morning operations, or to keep the water hot for another emergency, or possibly for both.

"Well, Ned, what is going to be the end of all this?" said Briscoe, walking up to me, after the storm of battle had subsided.

"I don't know," I replied. "We must wait and see what Tommy does. Of course we are ready to obey any reasonable orders."

"I am not exactly sure of that, after what has happened. Suppose the major wishes us to mareh back to Middleport. Shall we go?"

"I suppose we must," I replied, rather dubiously. "As both of us happen to be suspended just now, I conclude that we have nothing more to do with this business."

We sheathed our swords by mutual eonsent, and seated ourselves on the fence at the side of the road to wait for the "moving of the waters."

"What are we to do?" asked Crampton, one of the privates in my company.

"I'm sure I don't know," I answered, laughing. "I am willing to obey all reasonable orders, and I suppose you ought to do the same."

"We are ready to stand by you," added Dunbold, a corporal of the first eompany.

"We have the majority," said Sergeant Langdon, suggestively.

"We don't want to make a row yet," continued Crampton. "There will be one about to-morrow noon, when we vote for offieers. You know the balloting is to come off then. It can only be postponed by a vote of the battalion."

"I am suspended from duty, and of course I haven't anything to say," I added.

"That's just my case," said Briscoe. "I would rather keep quiet till after the election."

It was evident to me that we were on the very verge of the long-expected mutiny. The president of the Lake Shore Railroad Company, and the major of the battalion, had ruled us with a rod of iron. We had borne it longer than we intended; and the present occasion, when we were beyond the reach of outside influences, seemed to be favorable for the final settle-ment of the matter. As students, we were the equals, in every respect, of Tommy Toppleton, and we were determined to make him treat us like gentlemen.

While Briscoe and myself were discussing the situation, Sergeant Hacker, one of the major's adherents, advanced towards us. He looked as though he had come upon a desperate mission, for his lips were compressed, his eyebrows knit, and his step very decided.

"Captain Briscoe."

"Sergeant Hacker."

"Major Toppleton orders you to march your company down the road," continued the messenger, pointing to the place where Tommy had halted.

"All right! I will do so," replied Briscoe.

The captain of the first company gave his orders, and his command moved off, leaving my company and the band opposite the house. Hacker returned to the major, but immediately appeared again with an order for me to join the main body with the mutinous portion of my company. Tommy looked wrathful and disgusted, as he always did when he had been thwarted in his purposes.

"I am glad that you have concluded to obey orders," said he, with an obvious sneer in his tone and manner, as I saluted him, after halting my company.

"I shall always be ready to obey any reasonable order," I replied, respectfully.

"Reasonable!" exclaimed he. "What do you mean by reasonable?"

"Involving anything which it is proper for the battalion to do," I replied.

"Who is to determine whether it is proper or not?" demanded Tommy.

"I should say that you were, in the first place, before you gave the order," I answered, careful not to provoke his anger.

"I should say there was a mutiny in the line," added the major. "I don't want to argue the matter now. When I give an order, I intend to be obeyed, whether you consider it reasonable or not."

I made no reply, and the little major looked as pompous as though the question had been forever settled. I thought we could all afford to wait until the next day at noon, when the election was to take place; for it was a sure thing, if the balloting was fairly conducted, that Tommy would be ousted from his position, and Briscoe elected in his place. The matter, so far as the chief command was concerned, was settled, and the only question which had not yet been determined was whether or not Tommy should be elected to some other office.

Jed, his father, and Clarissa had taken position in the middle of the road, where they could observe the movements of the battalion. They were evidently willing that we should continue our march, and I hoped Tommy would be sensible enough to adopt this course, though it was expecting rather too much of him to permit his enemy to remain unpunished for a single day. He wheeled the battalion into line, and capered the sorrel pony along a couple of times in front, glancing fiercely from his warriors to the enemy before the house, apparently doubtful in regard to his next move. Finally he halted, and it was evident that he intended to make a speech.

"Fellows, I have been insulted!" said he, savagely. "Shall it be said that the whole battalion was beaten back by two men and two women?"

"The whole battalion was not beaten back," retorted Corporal Dunbold.

"Silence in the ranks!" exclaimed the major. "Will you stand by me, or not?"

"We will!" shouted Tommy's adherents; but the rest of the line said nothing.

"I thought you would. I was not willing to believe that my fellows would desert me when I wanted them most. I'm going to give that Jed a mauling; if I don't, there will be some bones broken somewhere."

Tommy was rapidly lashing himself into a fury, and would soon be in condition to undertake a desperate enterprise. I did not think he would face the hot water again; but the foe still stood in the road, seemingly unconscious of peril, and the sight of them was raising the major's blood to the boiling point. What could he do? Being only a boy myself, though I claimed to be a gentleman at the same time, I was curious to see the issue of the adventure, while I was firmly resolved to take no part in it, even if I was court-martialed, and dismissed the service for disobedience.

Ever since the battle on the Horse Shoe, Tommy had been in favor of flank movements. Wolf Penniman, though no soldier, had taught him a lesson in tactics which he had not learned before. In fact, Wolf seemed to have the tact to manage almost any difficult case. I saw the major survey the locality of the barn, in the rear of the house, and the fields adjoining. I had no doubt he was planning a diversion.

"Captain Skotchley, you will march your company through this field to the rear of the barn, and there await further orders," said Tommy, addressing me, with a flourish of his sword to point out the lot through which I was to pass.

The field indicated was green with new wheat, and

to march through it would be to inflict serious injury upon the farmer. I at once came to the conclusion that the order was an unreasonable one.

"That is a wheat field, Major Toppleton," I mildly suggested, though I knew very well that my remark would have no weight with the headstrong young magnate.

"What of it?" demanded he.

"Marching through that field will damage the wheat."

"I don't care if it does! It belongs to this old farmer, whose son insulted me. He takes his son's part, and he must also bear the consequences."

"But he can prosecute you in the court for trespass, and make you pay the damage."

"I don't care for the damage. I'm going to be even with that fellow before I leave this place."

"I would rather not take part in doing this mischief," I replied.

"I suppose you mean to say that my order is an unreasonable one."

"I did not put it in just that form, but that is what I mean."

"I suspended you once, Captain Skotchley."

"I am aware that you did."

"As you obeyed my next order, I was going to let it pass, and say nothing more about it," said Tommy, biting his lips.

"I will obey any and every order which comes within the line of my duty."

"A soldier should obey his superior without any question," retorted the major.

"Not always," I replied.

"Yes, always!" exclaimed Tommy, fiercely.

"Suppose the colonel of the regiment, in a time of peace, should order one of his captains to shoot ten men of his company," I suggested, calling up a sup- position which had been used in the lecture-room of the Institute.

"That is not a supposable case."

"The colonel might be attacked with sudden in- sanity."

"Do you mean to say I am insane?"

"I did not say anything of the kind. Our lecturer on military tactics was willing to grant that there could be instances when the inferior was not bound to obey the superior — nay, where it was his duty to disobey him."

"If there are such cases, this is not one of them," growled Tommy.

"I think it is. The battalion is out upon a tour of camp duty; and in everything relating to that I will obey orders. But I won't have anything to do with avenging fancied insults."

"Then you think that pulling me off my horse, and pitching me into the dirt, is only a fancied insult?" sneered Tommy.

"That was only part of the affair," I replied. "You ought to prosecute the man in court. You have no right to take the law into your own hands."

"Shut up!" snapped Tommy, as he rode away from me in disgust.

CHAPTER VI.

THE BATTLE IN THE WHEAT FIELD.

TOMMY had been talking with Haven, the first lieutenant of Company A, who was a reckless and unprincipled fellow, and it was probable that he had indicated a plan by which Jed might be properly punished for his temerity. The order I refused to obey directed me to march to the rear of the barn, and there await further instructions. The next command would have been to capture the fiery colt, pull down the cow-shed, or assault the hens and chickens — something to make a row which would divert the attention of the farmer's family, and call them to the scene of action. Then the first company would doubtless have been ordered to march up to the front of the house, empty out the hot water in the wash-boiler, capture the garden syringe, and lie in wait for the awful Jed.

Major Toppleton rode up to Briscoe, and repeated the order he had given to me. Of course the captain of the first company refused to obey. He was a sensible fellow, and knew that boys who were merely playing soldier would not be justified in doing mischief which could only have been tolerated in time of war, upon urgent necessity. Tommy was as much in earnest as though the country had been invaded by a warlike host, and its salvation depended upon the energy of his movements.

"Captains Briscoe and Skotchley are suspended from further duty, and will consider themselves under arrest," said the little major, pompously. "They shall be tried by court martial when we halt at noon to-day."

Tommy then gave his order to march to the rear of the barn to Faxon, the first lieutenant of my company. He followed my example, and Barnscott was placed in command. He was ready to obey any orders, no matter what they were. He would have set the barn on fire, if Tommy had told him to do so. He gave the necessary commands for moving the company towards the field, but only the twenty-five who had obeyed him before were willing to do so now. Tommy stormed, and even swore, after the manner of his father in such emergencies; but the rest of the company, thirty-five in number, were as resolute as their suspended officers, and refused to move into the field.

The moment the fellows began to leap over the fence, the old man and Jed rushed forward to prevent the mischief. They yelled with a vigor which did credit to their lungs, and, with clubs in their hands, placed themselves in the way of the advancing column. They were not content merely to stand before the troops; but they commenced a furious attack upon them with the sticks in their hands. Though bayonets are generally awkward weapons to run upon, the old man and his son did not seem to hold them in terror.

Tommy, furiously excited by this actual warfare, ordered the first company to march to the front of the house. At this movement Clarissa rushed into the house; but she presently appeared with the old lady, bearing the boiler of hot water. The women were quite as belligerent as the men, and a few dippers of hot soap suds compelled the brave boys of

Company A to retreat into the road again. But Haven, the master spirit of mischief, led his hot-water-battered forces over the fence above the house into the farmer's garden, and moved towards the rear of the barn, doing no little damage to beets, carrots, cabbages, and peas.

In the mean time, the old man and his son were fighting a very unequal battle with Company B — two against twenty-five. In the struggle, the young wheat was trodden down, and the ground torn up by the feet of the combatants. Briscoe and I were appalled at the probable consequences of the strife. A thrust of a bayonet might kill Jed or his father; while, at the best, our fellows were making fearful havoc in the grain field.

"Skotchley, this is rascally!" exclaimed Briscoe.

"I know it," I replied, with no little feeling, for I was disgusted with the strife.

"I don't know but we are just as guilty in looking on as we should be if we took part in it. I am willing, for one, to go in and stop this thing."

"So am I."

"We are going to stop this thing, fellows!"

shouted Briscoe, with energy. "Will you stand by us?"

"Yes, yes!" replied the line.

"Hold on a minute, Briscoe," I interposed, as a bright thought flashed upon my mind. "Where is Fryes?"

"Here he is. Fryes!" called Briscoe.

"Blow the retreat," I added, as the leader of the band presented himself, with his bugle in his hand.

Although this was not exactly a piece of infantry tactics, we had practised it in our studies, and the bugle call was well known to all the troops. Indeed, we had been taught the drill and evolutions of all arms of the service. Fryes blew the refrain, and it was heard by both of the companies, or rather the fragments of them which were in the field and behind the barn. Tommy, being on his horse, had been unable to follow either detachment to the service upon which he had ordered them. The troops who were engaged with the farmer and his son, in the wheat field, appeared to receive the bugle blast as a welcome sound, for, without waiting for any orders from their officers, they made haste to get over the fence into the road. The conflict had begun to flag in this quarter, and our fellows were certainly getting the worst of it.

I do not wish to have it understood that this fighting was very perilous to either party, for both took particular care to keep out of each other's way. It was simply running up and running back again, though one or two of our boys got a rap from the stick in the hands of Jed. If the conflict had continued a few moments longer, I think they would have been driven out of the field. But I was afraid some accident would happen to somebody.

By the time the second company had scaled the fence, the other appeared, coming at the double-quick towards the road, without any regard to the safety and future welfare of young beets, cabbages, and other garden vegetables. Major Tommy began to fly around on his little steed, for I learned that he had just sent a message to Haven, in the rear of the barn, to march into the wheat field, and take the old man and his son in the rear, intending to surround and capture them. Of course, when he saw his carefully laid plan, defeated, he was angry and excited, as usual.

"Who blew that retreat?" demanded he, fiercely, as he galloped his steed up to the place where Fryes stood.

"I .did," replied the chief musician, blandly.

"What did you do that for?"

"I was trying my bugle."

"Trying your bugle! I will give you a lesson before I have done with you."

"A lesson on the bugle?" asked Fryes.

"None of your impudence!" exclaimed Tommy, flourishing his sword as though he intended again to inflict corporal chastisement upon the musician.

But the little major did not mean anything of the kind. Rash as he was, he had a certain degree of prudence which did not permit him to hit the wrong person. If Tommy had struck him again, he would have been on the ground in the twinkling of an eye; for Fryes was a high-spirited fellow, who would not endure a second blow, especially from Tommy, whom he despised as a tyrant.

"I beg your pardon if I said anything impudent, major. I only answered your question," replied Fryes, with his usual gravity.

"Don't you blow that bugle again without orders from me."

The leader of the band did not even suggest that he had received an order from me to sound the retreat. He was always willing to take the responsibility; but Briscoe and I were ready to share it with him.

"Barnscott!" called the major.

The lieutenant of the second company, who had gathered his weary warriors near the spot where I stood, marched up to the major, and saluted him. He was still out of breath with the violence of his exertions in the field, or rather with the haste of his retreat, for his party had been closely pursued by the old man and his son.

"March your company back, and don't mind the bugle again."

"Major Toppleton, this thing has gone far enough," said Briscoe, stepping up to the little major.

"What do you mean by that, Briscoe?"

"I mean to say, for one, that I won't stand by any longer and see the farmer's crop destroyed."

"I say it, for another," I added.

"So say we all of us!" shouted the fellows in the line who had supported Briscoe and myself.

"Do you command this battalion?" demanded Tommy.

"I command some of it," answered the senior captain.

"And I command some more of it," I added.

"What are you going to do about it?" continued Tommy, angrily.

"We are going to protect the farmer," replied Briscoe.

"I should like to see you do it!" said Tommy, shaking his head. "You have your orders, Barnscott."

Tommy rode up to the other company, which had halted in the road on the front of the house, evidently for the purpose of sending it back of the barn again.

"Skotchley, you have thirty-five men, and I have only thirty," said Briscoe, beginning now to be excited by the job we had jointly undertaken. "You look out for Company A, and I will look out for Company B. Let's not have a fight, if we can help it."

"All right. I will do the best I can," I replied.

Briscoe was a veteran, for he had been the leading spirit in the battle on the Horse Shoe. With a few hasty orders, and a sharp movement, he placed his men between Barnscott's command and the wheat field. At the same time, I marched my men up towards the garden fence.

"Halt!" shouted Tommy, as he saw what I intended to do. "Why don't you halt when I tell you?"

We concluded not to halt, and reached the position to which Briscoe had assigned us. Fryes had followed me, for we were the best of friends. I think, if he had not kept an eye on the major, the irate commander would have pitched into me. We were now in the order of battle, both above and below the house; but I hoped that Tommy would not proceed to extremities, in the face of so many difficulties.

CHAPTER VII.

TOMMY YIELDS A POINT.

THE situation was not favorable to the success of Tommy's project. Briscoe and I had moved our companies with so much celerity that we had the "inside track." The major himself and his adherents appeared to be in a measure paralyzed by our sudden operations; and we had placed our men between the assailants and the objects of their ire. We were fully determined to prevent any further trespass upon the premises of the farmer. I must repeat, too, that all the better portion of the battalion were in our ranks; for it will readily be understood that Tommy's force consisted only of his toadies, — in short, of those who had not pluck enough to array themselves in opposition to the little major's tyranny.

We did not expect to be called upon to fight those who still adhered to Tommy's cause. We knew they had not the courage to attack us in earnest. For my own part, I intended simply to head them off if they attempted to enter the farmer's garden again. We were superior in numbers, as we were in spirit; and we could have closed with our opponents, man for man, taken them in our arms, and borne them away from the field of strife.

Jed had come out to the house to see what was going on there, when the marauders abandoned the field of wheat. The old man still remained there. Jed was not in good humor, and, as he approached the place where my command was posted, he manifested a disposition to break things, and I was not sure that he would not pitch into us, not comprehending the nature of the combination in his favor. The women still stood by their wash-boiler, in battle array.

"Now you can make tracks!" shouted Jed, as he approached me, with clinched fists, and a wrathful expression on his red face.

"I should like to speak to you a moment, if you please," I began, in a respectful way.

"I don't want any talk with you! You've done

mischief enough, and somebody's got to pay for it. If you don't travel pretty soon, there'll be some bones broken round here."

"I have done the best I could to save you from trouble, Jed. I have placed my men here to prevent any of the fellows from coming into your grounds."

"Is that so?" asked Jed, opening his eyes.

"You saw that the greater part of the battalion refused to attack you."

"Well, I did see that some of them hung back."

"More than half of them. Briscoe, down there, will not let any one into your wheat field, and I will keep them out of your garden."

"I wish you had begun sooner, then."

"We didn't know what the major meant to do till he did it."

"I'm going to cowhide that major."

"I wouldn't attempt to do anything of the kind," I continued. "He is the son of Major Toppleton, of Middleport. His father will pay for the damage his son has done, if you let the matter rest where it is."

"No, sir! I won't do it! I will take it out of his hide. You haven't any right to go marching about the country scaring horses. I'm going to wallop that young cub, and teach him manners."

"We did the best we could to stop the band, and we did stop it for a time, till we thought you had the colt where you could handle him," I explained.

"I don't find any fault with you, if you have done this; but that little popinjay on the pony don't get off without a thrashing, if I'm able to give him one; and I reckon I can lick the whole crowd of these boys."

"I advise you to keep quiet; make up your damages, and send the bill to Major Toppleton."

"No; I'm going to thrash that young cub," added Jed.

"We can't stand by and let you whip our chief officer. We will keep him from doing you any further damage; but you must let him alone."

"I don't know about that," said Jed, shaking his head.

By this time, the old farmer, seeing that no further mischief was likely to be done to the wheat field, came up to the house. He and Jed talked together; and the latter, perhaps counselled to do so by his father, refrained from his threatened attack upon Tommy. Everything was quiet along the line. Our intervention seemed to be an entire success. Tommy was in a quandary, and was holding a consultation with Haven, his right-hand man, on the other side of the street. The situation looked trying and difficult to him, without any doubt, and his principal adviser seemed to be unable to afford him any relief. They were discussing the matter very earnestly, and there appeared to be some difference of opinion between them. I judged that Tommy wanted to fight it out on that line, while Haven was disposed to defer the final settlement to a more fitting season.

We waited patiently for the result of this interview, though Faxon, the first lieutenant of Company B, agreed with me that there was little danger of the renewal of the conflict. When we were getting a little tired of the delay, a messenger came to me, and said that Lieutenant Haven desired to confer with Briscoe and myself. I was willing to meet him, and was curious to know what he had to say; but the captain of the first company refused to leave his command unless Barnscott's force was ordered away from the vicinity of the wheat field.

In answer to this objection Tommy graciously ordered the detachment of Barnscott to join that of
Haven, which was posted near me. I was not quite
satisfied with this arrangement, for it placed a force
of sixty in a situation to charge upon me the instant
negotiations failed. I therefore requested Briscoe to
place his command within supporting distance of me,
which he did. Jed and his father had seated themselves on a log before the house, and appeared to be
watching the proceedings with curiosity and interest.

Briscoe and I met Haven in the middle of the
road, between the two divisions of the battalion,
where each could repair to his command if there was
any alarm. Tommy sat upon his horse at a little distance from the spot, looking glum and dissatisfied.
I was rather surprised that he took the matter so
tamely. I concluded that Haven, who was an adroit
and cunning fellow, had some plan of his own which
he intended to carry out. Probably the approaching
election had some influence with both of them.

"I am directed by Major Toppleton to confer with
you in regard to your intentions," said Haven, looking from Briscoe to me.

"We have sufficiently indicated our intentions already, I think," replied Briscoe. "We did not come out on this trip for the purpose of injuring the property of the farmers. After Major Toppleton's blazing speech this morning about behaving like gentlemen, we didn't expect to see him making war upon wheat fields and gardens."

"If you think it is all right for a clown to pull the major from his horse, and pitch him into the dirt, you are welcome to your opinion. I don't think so," retorted Haven. "I'm willing to stand by my commander when he is abused, and I don't think much of any fellow who isn't."

"You are as welcome to your opinion as I am to mine. The major was wrong from the beginning."

"We won't talk about that," added Haven, with a sneer. "I only want to know what you are going to do."

"We are going to do what we think is right."

"What do you think is right?" inquired the ambassador. "Do you think it is right to get up a mutiny in the battalion?"

"I do, when the commanding officer so far forgets

himself as to trespass upon private property," replied Briscoe.

"Major Toppleton proposes to march back to Middleport," added Haven, evidently thinking this threat would bring us back to our senses.

"Very well," answered Briscoe.

"Do you intend to obey an order to that effect?" demanded the messenger.

Briscoe looked at me, as if he was in doubt. I was certainly undecided.

"I am not prepared to answer that question without consulting others," replied the senior captain, choosing the safe course.

"We will obey an order to march in the direction of Hitaca," I interposed. "When Major Toppleton comes back to his duty, we will obey him in all things as usual; but we will not be used in trampling down anybody's garden."

"I agree entirely with Captain Skotchley," said Briscoe.

"You seem to have taken the affairs of the battalion wholly into your own hands," sneered Haven.

"I haven't anything further to say," replied Briscoe, with dignity.

"I will report what you say to Major Toppleton," said the messenger, sourly, as he turned and walked away to the spot where Tommy was impatiently waiting the result of the parley.

The report of the ambassador was not likely to be satisfactory to the major. We were soon able to see that it was not so. A long and earnest discussion between Tommy and his right-hand man ensued. Haven was evidently counselling that discretion which is the better part of valor, or there could have been no difference of opinion between them. It was hard for the little magnate to yield a point, even for a time. His own friends would not be willing to abandon the tour of camp duty.

"What do you think he will do?" asked Briscoe.

"I don't know; but I am certain that you and I must be punished for what we have done," I replied.

"I don't intend to be punished," added Briscoe. "We have the majority on our side, and we can have it all our own way if we choose."

"I am in favor of obeying orders when they are proper."

"So am I."

"Here comes Haven again. I suppose something more is to be said," I continued, as the messenger again advanced towards us.

The lieutenant came up to us, and saluted in military form. I sincerely hoped that he had a message of peace.

"Major Toppleton directs me to say that he is entirely dissatisfied with your proceedings," Haven began. "He says that he shall hold the two captains responsible for their own disobedience, and for encouraging mutiny on the part of the men. He is unwilling to disappoint those who have faithfully obeyed his orders, or he would march the battalion back to Middleport. He desires to have it understood that his present action will not save the offenders from future trial and punishment. At his own convenience he will order a court martial."

Briscoe smiled, and so did I, as Tommy's favorite idea came up to the surface again. We were to be the victims of a court martial, after all! Haven saluted again, turned squarely on his heel, and walked back to the major's position.

CHAPTER VIII. .

THE FIRE IN THE FARM-HOUSE.

TOMMY TOPPLETON had certainly done what I had never known him to do before — he had yielded a point. Though he distinctly stated, through his messenger, that he held Briscoe and myself responsible for the trouble, and intended to court-martial us 'at the first convenient opportunity, he had still abandoned his position ; for, as nearly as I could judge by appearances, he intended to continue the march, and let the obdurate young farmer rest in peace for the present.

"Attention — battalion !" shouted the major, after a short conference with his right-hand man.

The fragments of the body obeyed the order, and gave attention ; but they did not form in single line, as usual. Tommy's adherents formed by themselves, and the mutinous portion did the same. The major gave an order to unite the discordant elements, and probably the order would have been obeyed if a third disturbing element had not at this moment appeared. My attention was attracted to the house by the screams of the old lady. I saw her rushing with frantic energy towards the open door, from which a volume of black smoke was issuing.

Jed and his father had been seated on a log for some time, watching the proceedings of the battalion. I suppose they did not wish to have the unequal conflict renewed, and doubtless Jed concluded that he had better profit by the good advice I had given. The two women had taken position near the men, and had watched our movements with interest and curiosity. The old lady appeared to have been the first one to discover the smoke. She was followed, in her rush to the scene of danger, by the two men and the pretty girl. As may well be supposed, all of them were alarmed, for the house was on fire.

Jed was the first to reach the door, and to enter the house, outspeeding his mother in the advance. He went in, but the dense volume of smoke was too much for him, and he was compelled to retreat. He came out rubbing his eyes, which were blinded by the smoke. Then his father rushed in at the open door; but he was driven back as hastily as his son had been. .

"Fire! Fire!" yelled Jed, when he had in some measure recovered from the effects of his visit to the interior of the house.

"Fire!" cried the old man.

The two women screamed; but none of the party seemed to have the presence of mind to do anything to stay the progress of the flames.

"This is a bad scrape!" exclaimed Briscoe. "We haven't seen the end of it. What shall we do?"

"Let us put out the fire," I replied.

"How shall we do it?" asked the senior captain.

"Throw on water. Stack arms, and send to the wagons for buckets!"

"Form companies!" shouted Tommy.

I looked at him. There was an evil expression of pleasure upon his face as he regarded the mass of smoke which issued from the door of the farm-house. He had not kindled the fire; but it was plain that he rejoiced to see it. He was ready now to march, and leave the devouring element to avenge the insult cast upon him. He was excited now, and issued his orders rapidly for the formation of the companies. While he was doing so, Briscoe marched his men — those only who had acted under him in the late conflict — to the side of the road, where he ordered them to stack arms. I followed his example. While we were thus engaged, Haven rushed up to us, and wanted to know if we did not intend to keep our promises. We had agreed to obey orders for the purpose of continuing the march.

"We are going to help put out the fire," replied Briscoe. "After that we will obey orders."

"You have nothing to do with the fire," replied Haven. "Major Toppleton orders you into line."

We gave no further attention to him, but directed our men to stack arms. Briscoe and myself led the way to the house, and all our friends followed. I closed the front door, and sent a squad of my company to the wagons for water-pails and other vessels.

"Come, Jed, bring out your pails, and everything else that will hold water! We can put this fire out in about three minutes," said I.

"Bring up that ladder!" called Briscoe to his force.

All the family, including the pretty girl, rushed to the back room, to the barn, and other parts of the premises, and soon appeared with buckets, tubs, kettles, pans, and other vessels. Briscoe's fellows raised the ladder to one of the second-story windows. There was a pump in the yard, and a brook crossed the road a short distance below the house.

"Now, Briscoe, if you will form a line to the brook and to the pump, I will take care of the water as fast as you bring it up."

"All right; but be in a hurry," replied the senior captain, who was more excited than I was.

By this time all the pails, tubs, and pans, from the wagons and from the house, were on the spot. I selected half a dozen reliable fellows to help me throw on the water. The lower part of the house was so full of smoke that it was impossible to go in. I went up the ladder, and entered the chamber above through the window. The fire was just working up through the floor, near the chimney.

"Pass up the water!" I called to those who had followed.

"Pass up the water!" repeated Faxon, at the window.

THE FIRE IN THE FARM-HOUSE. Page 86.

At this moment Jed joined me in the chamber. He had partially recovered his self-possession.

"What shall I do?" he asked.

"Get an axe, and cut a hole through the floor here where the fire is coming through."

He went to the window, and asked his father to send him an axe. The smoke in the room was becoming very dense; but the first bucket of water now appeared, and I poured it upon the spot where the flame was struggling through the floor. The pails came up now as rapidly as I could dispose of them. The axe was sent up, and Jed chopped away an aperture, so that I could throw the water down into the room below.

In a couple of minutes we had produced a decided impression upon the fire, and we had soon put out all the flames we could see. Leaving Faxon to pour on the water in the chamber, I descended by the ladder to the ground, with the intention of getting into the room below. I wished to see where the fire was, and to assure myself that it was not spreading in a direction where we had not reached it. I opened the door, and went in. I could remain but an instant;

but a single glance was enough to enable me to comprehend the situation.

There was a great pile of chips, shavings, and pine wood by the side of the stove, which had been brought in to heat the oven in the afternoon, as the old lady told me afterwards, when the "men folks" had gone to work. In the absence of the family, who had remained in the yard to watch the movements of the battalion, the heap of combustible matter had taken fire. The flames had been communicated to the woodwork, and were rapidly forcing their way upward.

The quantity of water which had been poured down from the chamber above had extinguished the fire in the partition, but it was spreading along the floor. Thus far the conflagration had been mainly confined to the heap of wood and shavings; for I assure the reader that it has taken much longer for me to relate the circumstances than it did for our fellows to do what has been described.

"Hold off above there, Faxon!" I shouted to my companion up stairs, as soon as I had rubbed the smoke out of my eyes.

"Is it all out?" demanded the lieutenant.

"No; but the water you throw on now does no good. Come down."

I took a bucket of water, rushed into the kitchen, and dashed it upon the burning pile. The effect was good; but I was obliged to retreat instantly. I hastily explained the situation to the group around me, and one after another a dozen fellows made a dive into the room, poured a pail of water on the fire, and then retired before the smoke had wholly blinded them. On my next visit to the scene of danger, I found that the fire had been nearly extinguished. I opened the doors and windows, so that the wind drove out the smoke. A few more buckets of water completed our work, and the family came in to see the effects of the fire.

The apartment was certainly in very bad condition, so far as appearances were concerned; but the damage was not very great. The wood-work around the chimney, and the floor near the stove, were burned away. The old man said that twenty-five or thirty dollars would repair the damages. The old lady declared that she never saw such a mess in her life.

"Well, who's to pay for all this?" said Jed, after the excitement had subsided.

"I don't know," I replied, glancing at my new uniform, which had suffered somewhat in the battle with the fire. "Do you think those who put the fire out for you ought to pay for it?"

"Well, no; I don't know 's I think so," replied he. "But it all come of your making such a row here — I mean the Toppleton boy. If he don't pay for it, I'll take it out of his hide."

"Captain Skotchley!" shouted Faxon, rushing into the house. "The major has taken all our guns, and is marching down the road with his fellows."

"What does that mean?" I inquired, astonished at this intelligence.

"I don't know; I suppose Tommy is going to bring us to terms," laughed Faxon.

"All right. Let him go. We will follow when we get ready."

"Are you sure the fire is all put out?" asked the old lady, anxiously.

"I think so," I replied; "but we can make sure of it before we go."

I went out doors, followed by Faxon. Our fellows were not a little excited by Tommy's last move, but Briscoe was quieting them. I ascended the ladder again, and entered the window, still attended by Faxon. There were no signs of fire in the chamber; but I thought it was possible that the flame had ascended within the wood-work, and I wished to examine the attic above. I soon found the stairs, and went up. Before I had reached the garret floor, I heard the step of a man. The door of the room over the chamber where we had poured down the water was suddenly closed, and I heard the springing of the bolt on the inside.

"There is somebody here," said Faxon.

"So I see," I replied, trying the door. "I heard the step of a man as we were coming up the stairs. There comes Jed."

"It's all right now," said the farmer's son. "Come down stairs, and I'll see to this."

"But the fire may have crept up here; and I hope you won't be burned up after we are gone."

"I'll see to that," replied Jed, anxiously.

"Who's in that room?"

"It's a man that used to work for us; he's crazy now," added Jed, placing himself between me and the door. "I will see to this room."

My curiosity prompted me to see the crazy man; but I could not insist, and I went down.

CHAPTER IX.

THE QUESTION OF RATIONS.

"WHAT does that mean, Faxon?" I asked, after we had left the house. "Do you suppose they keep a crazy man up in the attic?"

"Jed says so."

"They didn't go up after him when the house was on fire."

"I don't believe he is very crazy. He knew enough to go into his room and bolt the door after him, when he heard us coming," answered Faxon.

"Why should Jed be so particular not to have us see him?" I inquired. "He seemed to be much troubled about it. Did you mind how careful he was to put himself between me and the door?"

"Yes; he didn't seem to feel just right about it, and was in a great hurry to have us go down stairs. The man goes about the house; so he can't be very bad. I shouldn't wonder if there was something wrong about it," added Faxon.

"What can be wrong about it?" I asked.

"I don't know. If it had been all right, Jed would not have cared so much about our seeing the crazy man."

By this time Jed had come down, and joined us in the yard. He looked awkward and embarrassed; and, as I saw him standing in front of the house, it recalled a circumstance which I had noticed at the beginning of the fire, but which at that time had no significance. I saw the old lady talking earnestly to her son, and pointing up to the attic window. Then Jed disappeared, and I did not see him again till I entered the chamber. I concluded that the woman was alarmed about the safety of the crazy man, and that Jed did something to save him in case the house should be destroyed. Indeed, none of the family had done anything to extinguish the flames at first, and I was now willing to give them credit for their humanity in attending to the safety of the unfortunate, instead of condemning them, as I had done, for their lack of energy and presence of mind in the trying emergency.

"This is a bad day's work for us," said Jed, with a kind of lugubrious expression on his sun-browned face.

"I'm sorry for it," I replied. "We ought to be thankful, however, that the matter is no worse, for your house came pretty near being burned up."

"I haven't any fault to find with you fellows who tried to get us out of the scrape; but if it don't cost that Toppleton boy something, it won't be my fault."

"How long have you had that crazy man up there?" I inquired.

"O, more than a year. He don't give us any trouble; but he gets wild when he sees strangers. That's the reason I didn't want him to see you."

"It's lucky he didn't get burned to death," said Faxon.

"I looked out for him in the first of it. I took him down into the shed; but, as soon as the fire was put out, I sent him back again, for fear he should see some of you, and have a fit on him."

"If he was up in that room, he must have seen some of us in the yard."

"Well, it don't seem to make any difference with him, if people don't come close to him."

But Jed did not appear to like the subject, and tried to avoid it. The curiosity we manifested increased his embarrassment, and several times he hinted to us that we had better resume our march. He declared that he must see to his colt; that he must go for the body of the wagon, which the crazy animal had left on the hill; and he must help the folks clean out the kitchen. But he did none of these things while we remained.

"I hope the fire will not break out again," I continued, as Faxon and I moved towards the place where Briscoe was talking with our boys.

"I don't think there is any danger."

"The fire may have worked its way up into the crazy man's room, and I advise you to keep a sharp lookout."

"I shall. I went into the room. There was some smoke there, but I couldn't find any fire," replied Jed, fidgeting as though he was afraid we should insist upon visiting that room.

We did not insist, and Faxon and I joined our

companions in the road; and we had no difficulty in turning our attention from the crazy man in the attic to the crazy boy in command of our battalion. Major Tommy had loaded the guns of our portion of the crops on the wagons, and departed in the direction of Hitaca. We were disarmed, and not in fighting condition. We concluded that our commander, in depriving us of our weapons, intended to bring us to terms.

As I approached, Briscoe came forward to meet me, and led me one side to consider the circumstances in which we were placed. He appeared to be much more annoyed than I was at the movement of Tommy. We had the cream of the battalion on our side, and I did not doubt our ability to recover our arms when we were so disposed.

"Well, Skotchley, what are we to do?" said he, rather anxiously.

"We may as well march till we come up with the rest of the battalion," I replied, laughing, in spite of myself, at the gravity of the senior captain.

"You seem to think it is a joke," he added.

"Rather of that order, I am inclined to believe."

7

"I don't think so. Tommy has all the arms."

"No matter for that."

"But what is worse, he has the wagons, which contain all our provisions. We can't get any dinner unless he pleases to give us some. He can starve us into subjection."

"I guess not," I added, amused at the idea.

"We may as well look at the thing as it is. How far is it from here to Priam, the next town on the road?"

"Seven or eight miles."

"If you ever went over this road, you must know that it is a rocky country before us, and there is hardly a house between here and Priam."

"I never went over the road."

"I think this is the last farm-house for several miles. We are on the border of a very rough region," continued Briscoe, earnestly.

"Well, what odds does that make? I don't care how rough it is. The scenery will be all the finer, and we shall enjoy the tramp the more."

"You make light of it, Skotchley; but I can tell you this — that Tommy has us on the hip."

"I don't see it."

"In a couple of hours more it will be dinner time. What are we going to do then?"

"Dine."

"You can't dine very well without something to eat."

"When we get hungry enough, we shall be ready to fight a battle for the sake of our stomachs. We can capture the baggage wagons then."

"Perhaps not," replied Briscoe. "We haven't a musket, and Tommy's crowd are well armed. They have the inside track."

"Then we can switch off."

"Switch off?"

"Yes, and take the inside track."

"Tommy isn't much of a schemer himself, though he is not without tact; but Haven, who is his principal adviser, is a good manager. In my opinion, instead of drilling with the Wimpletonians, we are going to have a war among ourselves."

"If we do, we shall bring Tommy to his senses before it is finished."

"If the major can keep us off till to-morrow noon,

he and his flunkies may elect officers to suit themselves."

"I don't think we are going to have any serious trouble. Tommy will hardly make war upon a majority of the battalion."

"Humph! He would make war on all the world! I have my doubts about going ahead any farther."

"O, don't back out!" I replied.

"I don't mean to back out; but I don't feel just right about marching our fellows down here without anything to eat. If Tommy finds a position where he can protect his camp, he may hold us at bay till our fellows are starved into compliance with his terms."

"I acknowledge that the ration question is a difficult one," I added.

"That's almost the only one. If we had the wagons, we could make our own terms."

"We can take the bull by the horns, then."

"Yes, if we can get hold of the horns."

"No trouble about that. Is there any money among our fellows?" I asked.

"I suppose there is."

"Money makes the mare go."

"What good will money do in the wilderness before us?"

"I'll give you my idea, Briscoe, and you can lay it before the fellows if you like."

"Go ahead, for I don't want to back out. Tommy has been our tyrant for two or three years. He has behaved badly to-day, and I think we have done right in trying to check him. We tried to save Jed's horse, we prevented Tommy's flunkies from doing any more mischief to the farmer's property, and we put out the fire when our commander would have permitted the house to be burned up. I think we have the right of the matter. I don't want to march back to Middleport, as we must if we have no provisions."

"We must take a stock of provisions with us," I suggested. "That's my plan."

"I never thought of that; but where are we to get them?" asked Briscoe, his face lighting up with hope.

"Buy them. We can pick up money enough among the fellows to purchase a week's supply, I think. We have eighty, and a quarter apiece will give us twenty dollars."

"Good!"

"We can hire Jed to go in his wagon, with one or two of us, to the store three miles back. We have the pots and kettles belonging to the camp equipage with us, and we can do our own cooking."

"That's a capital idea, Sketchley, and I feel better already. But we have no tents."

"No matter; the fellows can sleep on the ground before a big fire; but my idea is, that we shall have the tents before we want to sleep."

Briscoe liked my plan very much, for it seemed to solve all the difficulties of the situation. We went over to the place where the two companies were, and the senior captain stated the case to them, declaring that we must either return to Middleport, or obtain a supply of provisions for the march. The boys were unanimously in favor of going ahead, and we "passed round the hat." Counting the proceeds of the collection, the result was over thirty dollars.

Jed was open to a trade; and for a dollar he agreed to convey Faxon, who was appointed commissary for the occasion, to the store. He brought out his colt, which now behaved in a very orderly manner, and attached him to the forward wheels of his wagon. Half a dozen of the boys went to the top of the hill where the body of his wagon was, to assist in mounting it. The party soon returned, and assured us that our agent was on his way to the store.

CHAPTER X.

WHO THE CRAZY MAN WAS.

OUR fellows were highly excited at the prospect of a contest with Tommy Toppleton and his minions. We believed that we had the right of way — that the track belonged to us; and the question was, which of us should "switch off." Our present plan provided against the perils of starvation, and everybody was good-natured.

"This does not look much like a prize drill on Friday — does it, Skotchley?" asked Briscoe, as we sat on the fence, waiting for the return of our commissary.

"Not much."

"We can't get round the lake by Friday, if we fool away our time in this manner."

"If we are behind time, we can take one of the steamers down the lake. But I am more afraid the battalion will be broken up, before Friday, by Tommy's obstinacy. If he don't come to terms —"

"What terms?" asked Briscoe, laughing.

"I don't know," I replied, "on precisely what terms we are to make peace; but we are to have a new major, and for one, I will no longer submit to Tommy's tyranny."

"So say we all of us."

"You will be chosen major, if we have a fair election; and if we don't have a fair one, we will not submit to it."

"Things look decidedly squally," added Briscoe.

"That's true; but if we can make our fellows stick, it will come out all right."

"O, they will stick. We have all the best fellows of the Institute on our side."

"They haven't any tyrant on the other side of the lake now."

"No. Isn't it odd? They say Waddie is a real gentleman. He don't put on airs, and don't even get mad."

"Wolf Penniman converted him. It's a great pity he can't convert his father."

"So it is; but I think we should be satisfied, on our side, if Tommy Toppleton could be converted into a decent fellow, though it won't be our fault if he is not."

"That's so," laughed Briscoe. "I suppose it would not be very hard for some of us to get transferred to the Wimpleton Institute, after the summer vacation, if things don't go right on this side."

"My father and Major Toppleton are old friends, and I found it rather hard for me to get away," I added. "But I hope Tommy will switch off, and get on the other track."

"I hope so. What's that?" exclaimed Briscoe, pointing up to the chimney of the farm-house nearest to us. "Isn't it smoke?"

"Yes, it is, as true as you live!" I replied, excited by the sudden prospect of another fire.

The old farmer and his family were still at work in the kitchen, cleaning out the wreck of the fire. After examining the casing of the chimney in the house, I had been fearful that some sparks had been drawn up into the wood-work above. If I had been permitted to look into the attic chamber where the crazy man lived, I could have determined whether there was any fire there or not. I doubt whether Jed went in at all.

"We must go to work again, Briscoe," I added, waiting for him, as my senior officer, to give me orders.

"You look out for the inside, and I will see that the water is passed up to you."

Taking Langdon and Dunbold with me, I ran into the kitchen, and told the people that the house was on fire near the roof. I did not wait to ask permission, but rushed up stairs, followed by my companions. I looked into the chamber where we had worked before, but there was no fire there. I ascended to the attic. The door of the crazy man's chamber was still fastened. It was possible that he was not yet aware of the presence of the devouring element so near him. Indeed, the smoke we had seen outside was so slight as hardly to attract our notice.

"Fire! Fire!" I shouted, pounding vigorously upon the door.

The crazy man took no notice of us, and I repeated the warning demonstration. By this time the old farmer had made his way up stairs. He rapped on the door several times, with no better success than had attended my appeal.

"Open the door," said the farmer. "The house is afire up here somewhere."

"No fire in here," replied the occupant of the room.

"Perhaps it's outside," suggested the old man, as he looked up to a scuttle in the roof, which I had not before noticed. "If one or two of you would go on the roof, you could see just where it is."

Corporal Dunbold, who was distinguished as a gymnast, offered to render this service. Placing a flour barrel on an old table, he reached the scuttle, opened it, and went out upon the roof. Sergeant Langdon followed him.

"If the house is on fire, you ought to get this man out," I suggested to the farmer.

"I suppose so. I must break the door down. He's very obstinate. You run down and get me the axe, and I'll break in the door."

I ran down stairs to the room below, where Jed had left the axe with which we had cut through the floor. When I was half way up the stairs on my return, I heard the door of the crazy man's chamber open. Somehow, I was not afraid of him, though I had been told that the sight of strangers made him violent. I reached the top of the stairs just as he came out of the room. The farmer was hurrying him towards the apartment on the other side of the entry; but I met him face to face.

The crazy man was Christy Holgate, who had robbed Wolf Penniman's father of twenty-four hundred dollars!

I saw him and recognized him, though he had grown very thin and pale since I had last seen him, more than a year before, on the steamer. Of course I was astonished at the sight of him, for it was generally believed in Middleport that the robber had fled to the South. For the moment, I forgot that I was looking for the fire; but the farmer hurried Christy into the other chamber, and presently joined me at the head of the stairs.

"Do you find any fire?" he asked, anxiously.

"Not yet," I replied, leading the way into the crazy man's chamber.

"There isn't any fire here," said the farmer. "I think it's a false alarm."

"We certainly saw some smoke rising from the roof, near the chimney, on the outside."

I put my hand upon the casing of the chimney. It was quite hot, and I was satisfied that it was not a false alarm. It was plain enough that the farmer's house would soon be enveloped in flames if the fire was not reached and checked. By this time, Briscoe had raised a long ladder to the attic window. Dunbold reported that the smoke was coming out through the cracks around the chimney.

"Pass up the water, fellows!" I called at the open window.

The boys were already on the ladder; and, as soon as I had a couple of buckets of water in the room, I directed the farmer to cut away the casing of the chimney; for I did not deem it prudent to admit the air till we were ready to fight the flames. He promptly struck a few vigorous blows with the axe, and down came the boards, charred on the inside by the fire. A few pails of water finished the work, though we did not leave the place till we had drenched the roof around the chimney. We poured in water till there was no longer any possibility of a secret spark doing any mischief.

The farmer, who seemed to take a more Christian view of our relations than his son did, was very grateful to us for the service we had rendered. He offered to give us all a dinner if we would wait long enough for his " women folks " to cook it. As we were in no particular hurry, we accepted the invitation. The old lady and Clarissa — who was a neighbor for whom Jed had a particular regard — went to work, boiling potatoes and frying bacon, at the stove in the midst of the ruins of the kitchen.

"Your man up stairs don't seem to be very crazy," said I to the farmer, while we were waiting.

"Only when he sees strangers."

"Why don't you send him to an asylum?"

"Well, he don't give us any trouble. When no one but our own folks are here he comes down to his meals. Besides, he's my wife's brother. He had some trouble a while ago, and that rather turned his head. He thinks somebody is after him all the time."

I did not wonder at this, for somebody had been

after him for weeks or months after he committed his crime. Wolf's father had been his best friend; and, while the steamer, of which Christy was the engineer, was lying at the wharf in Ucayga, he had taken Mr. Penniman's pocket-book from him. When he was discovered, he attempted to escape on a locomotive; but Wolf jumped on with him, and, by the aid of a pistol he had taken from Waddie Wimpleton, compelled him to give up the pocket-book. He gave it up; but he had taken the twenty-four hundred dollars from it. He took to the woods, and the sheriffs could not find him. Probably he had been concealed all this time at his sister's house. I wondered where the money was, the loss of which had nearly ruined Wolf's father.

I did not deem it wise to inform the farmer that I had recognized Christy in the crazy man. It was possible that a portion of the money might yet be recovered, and persons more skilled than I was in such matters ought to manage the case. Wolf's steamer touched at Priam, which lay in our route, and I decided, if I could not see "the young captain" there, to leave a note for him.

It was nearly twelve o'clock when Jed and Faxon returned with the wagon well loaded with provisions, such as crackers, shipbread, bacon, salt fish, potatoes, and other articles which we could conveniently use. Our dinner was now nearly ready, and all the resources of the farm-house were required to feed us. There were knives and forks enough for only a small portion of our company; but, as we were used to camping out, and realized that "fingers were made before forks," we had no difficulty in filling our stomachs.

Jed had become very good-natured, for Faxon had explained to him the particulars of the difficulty between the two divisions of the battalion. He hoped the Toppleton boy would be whipped out, and he would be willing to go down and help us do it. We did not need any assistance of this kind; but, when he volunteered to convey our provisions and stores down to Priam, we accepted his offer; but he harnessed the colt's mother for this service.

At one o'clock we took up the line of march. As we felt that we were going to battle, Briscoe sent scouts ahead to warn us of the presence of the enemy.

CHAPTER XI.

IN THE WILD REGION.

IT looked to me just as though another war of the students had actually commenced, not between the rival academies this time, but between different factions of the same institution. But this statement of the case did not exactly suit me, for I felt that I had no quarrel with my fellow-students; and it was more reasonable to call it a rebellion against the tyranny of Tommy Toppleton. The question was whether Tommy, who was only the equal of his fellow-students, should treat them like inferiors; should bully them, snub them, and, at his lordly mandate, compel them to invade a farmer's wheat field, trample down his garden, and assault his people.

I thought not, and so thought a majority of us. Our remedy was to elect a new major — one who would be reasonable; one who, while he required strict obedience to his legitimate military commands, would treat us like officers and gentlemen; one who would not make war on the gardens, chicken coops, and barns of the farmers through whose territory we were to pass. Most of us were satisfied that in Captain Briscoe we should find such a person, and a majority of us intended to place him in this high position.

Major Tommy had deprived us of our arms, and continued the march with the wagons containing the tents, provisions, and other stores. But, we had plentifully supplied ourselves with eatables, so that we could not be starved into subjection. I feared that Tommy, who, whatever he might say on the subject, was disturbed about the result of the approaching election, would dispose of the matter with the minority, who still adhered to his fortunes. The battalion headquarters were with him; the roster and records were in his possession, or in that of the sergeant-major, who was one of his toadies; so that an election conducted by him would be technically legal, though really unfair and unjust.

In regard to the major's mode of operations we were

still in the dark. We had about eight miles of wild country before us, abounding in forests, headlong steeps, deep ravines gored in the stupendous rocks, in rushing torrents, and lofty cascades. Later in the season this region was visited by thousands of tourists, and at Priam there was a large hotel for their accommodation. At the present time we were not likely to be disturbed; for, though a good road extended through this picturesque territory, it was but little used, for nearly all the travel between Middleport and Priam was done by the steamboats on the lake.

We marched from the farm-house, where so many lively incidents had occurred, and entered the wild region. There was no one to molest or make us afraid. Having no arms to carry, we had an easy time of it. Of the twenty members of the band and drum corps, we had fifteen, and occasionally Fryes gave us a tune to enliven the march. Our scouts led the way a mile in advance of us, to notify us of any hostile demonstration on the part of Tommy's adherents, who were at least three hours ahead of us. Occasionally we halted at the mountain torrents which flowed down the rocks, or dashed along by the side of the road, to refresh ourselves with a draught of the pure water; but we saw neither man nor beast. Not even a stray tourist had anticipated the season, though many sportsmen had come up to fish on the lake.

"This isn't very bad — is it?" said Briscoe, halting at the road-side till I came up with him.

"No; it's a beautiful country," I replied. "I wouldn't mind spending a week or two among these rocks."

"I should like it first rate; and I wonder we have never come up here to camp out," added the senior captain.

"The country is not very favorable for camps and military evolutions."

"That's so; there's hardly room enough to pitch our tents on any one spot."

"I wonder where Tommy is," continued Briscoe. "I expected to come up with him before this time."

"Some of our fellows say that Haven knows all about this wild region, and I suppose he is conducting Tommy's forces. What do you suppose they mean to do?"

"I have no idea of the particular way in which they intend to manage the business; but Tommy means to have himself elected major without any help from us. He must know by this time that we shall not vote for him."

"Perhaps he means to hide in the hills till after noon to-morrow, and then come out to tell us he has been elected major," I suggested. "Of course you and I will be elected high privates, for Tommy's fellows will have all the best places — all the commissions at least, if not all the warrants. Then we are to be court-martialed, and punished as he thinks we deserve."

"But he can't carry on an election without a quorum," said Briscoe. "The rules require that one half shall be present to do any business."

"I fancy he will find some way to get over this difficulty."

"I don't see how he can get over it. He has only sixty-five, including the three wagon-masters."

"He has always been a law unto himself, and I don't see why he shouldn't be in this instance."

"Are all our fellows true-blue?" asked Briscoe, in

a low tone, and with some anxiety apparent on his face.

"I suppose they are," I answered. "Of course there are some who don't care much how the thing goes."

"I was thinking that Tommy, if we should get together again, might find means to win some of our fellows over on his side. If he could draw over about a dozen of them, that would give him a quorum. Then, if he could keep us at a distance, he might elect every officer to suit himself."

"We must explain the matter to our fellows, and fortify them."

"That's so; we will do it next time we halt."

Briscoe resumed his place at the head of the column, and we continued the march till an inviting brook induced him to halt for a drink. We had plenty of drinking vessels with us, which we had used in putting out the fire. Like all boys, our party were thirsty every time they saw a good chance to drink. But, before they had satisfied themselves, two of the four scouts who had led the advance, one of whom was Faxon, were seen hastening towards us. It was evident that some important discovery had been made.

Of course Tommy's movements had been the subject of constant discussion among our party, and all sorts of opinions were expressed in regard to his course. Some thought he would not halt till he reached Priam, where he would send for his father to sit in judgment upon the rebels. Others believed he would hide himself in the woods, and ascertain what our party intended to do. But the prevailing opinion was, that he intended to starve us into yielding to all his requirements. Perhaps they thought so because this was the very emergency for which we had so carefully provided.

Lieutenant Faxon and Corporal Dunbold were the two scouts who returned to the main body. Both of them looked excited, if not anxious, as they approached, and we concluded that the solution of Tommy's intentions was at hand. Our fellows at once forgot that they were thirsty, and hurried away from the brook to meet the scouts, and obtain the latest tidings of the major's operations.

"What is it, Faxon?" demanded Briscoe, striving

to keep cool, and thus maintain the dignity of the commanding officer of the rebels — for such we acknowledged that we were, and quoted the example of the patriots of the Revolution to sustain our position.

"Tommy and his forces have halted on High Bluff," replied Faxon, out of breath with the haste he had made.

"What's High Bluff?" asked a dozen of our party.

"What are they doing?" inquired a dozen more.

"Are they going to fight?" demanded others.

"Well, I can't answer a dozen questions at once," replied Faxon, laughing, as he seated himself on a rock to rest his weary limbs.

"Order!" shouted Briscoe. "Fall back! Rest yourself a minute, Faxon, and I will form the line, and have the business done without interruption."

The senior captain and myself ordered our two companies to form a line, telling them that any disorder might lose us the battle. They were reasonable enough to see the point.

"Now keep in line, fellows. I will tell you all about it as soon as I ascertain the situation," said Briscoe.

"All right!" shouted the students.

"No soldier will leave the line without orders. As soon as I find out where Tommy is, I will tell you what we will do."

Certainly our troops were very well disciplined; for, impatient as they were, not one of them left his place. Leaving Lennox in charge of the line, Briscoe and I hastened to the place where Faxon was resting himself.

"I think Tommy has us in a tight place," said the scout, as we seated ourselves in front of him.

"Why so? What has he done?" asked Briscoe, rather nervously.

"He has camped on High Bluff, and pulled up the bridge, so that we cannot reach him."

"I don't know anything about High Bluff," added Briscoe, impatiently.

"Some folks call it Bellevue. It is a kind of promontory on the shore, which commands a beautiful view of the lake and its eastern borders."

"What bridge has he pulled up?" inquired Briscoe, still unable to comprehend the situation.

"The bridge over the ravine at High Bluff. It

was built by the hotel-keeper at Priam, so that his guests could drive upon the promontory, and get the view there without leaving their carriages."

"But what's the need of a bridge if the bluff is on this side of the lake?" I asked.

"On each side of the promontory there is a wide gully; or, in fact, they are two arms of the lake. Between the bluff and the road there is another gully, through which flows the brook, which is there almost a river. Indeed, the two arms of the lake are the two mouths of this stream, and the bluff is an island."

We understood his explanation, and were satisfied that Major Tommy had chosen a strong position in which to subdue the rebels.

CHAPTER XII.

BEFORE HIGH BLUFF.

"WHAT does Tommy intend to do?" asked Briscoe. "What is he going to make by fortifying himself on High Bluff?"

"I don't know," answered Faxon. "Of course he don't know that we have anything to eat, and I suppose he thinks he can starve us till we submit or clear out."

"I think we will not let him know that we have anything in the way of provisions," added Briscoe.

"Probably he means to keep us out of our guns also," I suggested.

"Isn't there any way to get on the bluff?" inquired Briscoe.

"I don't know of any way. On the two arms of the lake the water is deep, and the sides of the promontory are nearly perpendicular."

"How deep is the ravine between the road and the bluff?"

"Fifteen or twenty feet, as nearly as I can remember; but the stream is a rushing torrent at the bottom of it," replied Faxon.

"Never mind; we will look at the place very soon. We can tell best how to proceed when we know what Tommy intends to do. Where are the other two scouts, Faxon?"

"I left them up by the bluff, to keep a lookout."

"That's right."

"I told them not to let any of the fellows on the bluff see them."

"Good!" exclaimed Briscoe. "As I understand the matter, Tommy can no more get out of his fortress than we can get into it."

"Not unless we permit him to relay the bridge he has taken up."

"We will take care of that. Now, is there any place for us to camp near the bluff, Faxon?"

"There is room enough above the road, though there isn't much chance to pitch many tents."

"We haven't many to pitch," laughed Briscoe.

"Now we must have a talk with our fellows, and see how they feel."

We walked up to the front of the line, where our boys were impatiently waiting to learn the nature of Tommy's position. The senior captain explained it to them, so that a portion of them probably understood it.

"I can't tell what we shall do till we are on the ground," said Briscoe. "One thing is certain: if Tommy's fellows will not let us on the bluff, we will not let them off; for it's a poor rule that won't work both ways."

"That's so!" laughed the crowd.

"We have plenty to eat. We can live comfortably for three days on our stock of provisions. Tommy will have the election to-morrow, I suppose; and very likely he will try to get some of you to go over and help him."

"Not much!" shouted some of the more enthusiastic of the rebels.

"If any of you wish to go, I shall not prevent you from doing so."

"We won't have anything to do with them!" exclaimed several.

"They can't elect officers without a quorum, which is half the battalion. If they can buy off, say, ten of you, they can do it — not without."

"We'll duck any fellow that deserts," cried private Crampton.

"That's the talk!"

"Fellows, I, for one, can't submit any longer to Major Toppleton's tyranny," continued Briscoe, warmly. "If any of you wish to do so, it is none of my business."

"We don't!"

"If we stick together, we can make an end of it before to-morrow night."

"Stick together!" yelled the crowd, with one voice.

"We are rebels now," laughed Briscoe.

"That's so!"

"But we must have good discipline, or we can't do anything," the senior captain proceeded. "If you are not satisfied with your present officers, choose others at once."

"No! No!"

"You are satisfied, then?"

"Yes! Yes!"

"Very well. If you want somebody else to command you, say the word, and I will cheerfully obey any one you may select."

"Briscoe forever!"

"Thank you. I wish you to obey orders without asking any questions. If you do, we shall come out all right."

"Briscoe and liberty!" screamed a facetious fellow.

"Briscoe — the Washington of the Toppleton Institute!" roared another.

"Briscoe — the next major of the battalion!"

"Thank you, fellows; but the less buncombe we have, the better we shall get along," interposed the recipient of all these honors.

Briscoe gave his orders to form in column, and the march was resumed. Jed, with the old mare, — the mother of the fiery colt, — brought up the rear with the provisions and stores. We were an excited band of warriors, for we expected a stirring time for the next day, if not for the coming night. For my own part, I was continually studying the problem which Faxon's description of High Bluff presented, in order to find the means of spanning the abyss that yawned between the two rival and opposing portions of the battalion. I was quite sure that, if Wolf Penniman had been with us, his engineering abilities would have enabled him to walk right over it. But he was not with us, and we should be compelled to overcome the difficulty ourselves.

"Halt!" said Briscoe, at the head of the column, after we had marched about a mile.

Stepping forward, I saw the two scouts, whom Faxon had posted in the road to observe the movements of Tommy's force during his absence. We could not yet see High Bluff, as it was concealed by the foliage of the trees.

"What are they doing, Langdon?" asked Briscoe of one of them, whom he had called from his station.

"Nothing but fixing up the camp," replied the scout. "Some of them are cooking their supper, and others are loafing about the bluff. I should judge that they had everything arranged to suit themselves. There are a couple of sentinels near the road, who seem to be looking out for us. You can go up there and take a look without being seen."

Briscoe and I walked forward till we obtained a

full view of High Bluff. The situation was substantially as Faxon had described it. The tents were pitched on the highest part of the promontory. The arms were stacked in front of them. Near the gully, the material of which the bridge had been composed was piled up. On one side, a party were engaged in cooking. The chasm between the road and the camp seemed impassable to me, for I was no engineer. I could not help commending Tommy for the good judgment he had displayed in choosing this natural fortress for his camp, though I could not see how he intended to carry his point.

"Have they seen you yet, Langdon?" asked Briscoe of the scout.

"No; I'm sure they don't know that we are within five miles of them."

"We may as well keep still, then. Don't you think so, Skotchley?"

"For the present, at least. Here is a good place to camp," I replied, pointing to a grove by the side of the road.

"That will be as good as we can find," he replied.

The spot was a perfect paradise of lovely scenery.

The ground, comprising about half an acre, was smooth. It was fenced in with picturesque rocks, except on the side nearest to the arm of the lake which separated it from High Bluff. All around and above us, the trees grew out of the crevices in the rocks. Into this shady retreat Briscoe marched our forces. Jed's wagon was unloaded, and its contents piled up in a convenient place.

"What are you going to do now?" asked Jed, after he had turned his mare, in readiness to return home.

"Probably we shall not do anything to-night," replied Briscoe.

"If I were you, I would go on that bluff, and clean them out before to-morrow morning," laughed Jed.

"How would you get over there?" I inquired.

"Come with me, and I'll tell you."

Jed led the way to the arm of the lake nearest to us. At the part adjoining the road it was not more than thirty feet wide. Pointing to a tall pine, he gave a significant nod.

"Don't you see it now?" he inquired, with a broad grin.

"No, I don't," replied Briscoe.

"You are not so smart as you were this fore-noon," laughed Jed. "Don't you see that you can cut that tree down, and let it drop over the gully, so as to make a bridge for you?"

"Cut it down! How? With a jackknife?"

"No, with an axe."

"We haven't any axe, in the first place; and in the second, if we had, we couldn't fell that tree in seven years."

"I can fetch that tree down in half an hour, as easy as I can turn my hand."

"We couldn't if we had a dozen axes,' added Briscoe.

"Well, see here; you have done us a good turn to-day, boys, and I'll bring down an axe and drop it for you."

"That's the idea!" exclaimed Briscoe. "We shall be ever so much obliged to you, if you will."

"I'll do it, and welcome."

"But we must not let them know on the bluff what we are about," I suggested.

"Certainly not," added Briscoe. "I see it all

The Camp on High Bluff. Page 133.

plain enough now. We will make a demonstration over by the road, as though we were going to throw a bridge across the chasm."

"That's the idea! The brush on the edge here is so thick that Tommy's fellows can't see what we are about until the pine falls. Then we will rush over on the tree, and capture the fortress."

Jed promised to be on the ground the next morning with his sharp axe, and then started for home. Briscoe and I surveyed the ground again. We could do nothing that night, and, if we kept out of sight, probably Tommy would think we had returned to Middleport in disgust. We were willing he should think so, and we instructed our fellows to keep as quiet as possible. But it was necessary to have a fire, in order to make coffee, for which we had brought with us all the materials. The smoke and the light were liable to betray us; but it was agreed all around that it would be better to be betrayed than do without the coffee.

Faxon, while at the store, had been thoughtful enough to provide a supply of tin cups. We had a can of milk in the cold water of the brook. Several

of our fellows were experienced in cooking, and if
we had supped with the Lord Mayor of London, we
could not have been better satisfied with the fare,
though we had only bread and butter and cheese.
And never were eighty-five young gentlemen happier,
or better pleased with themselves, than we were. It
was the night before the battle; but we were content to wait, though, as it happened, the battle commenced that night, and very soon after we had finished
our supper. Perhaps it was just as well, for the
coffee was rather trying to our nerves, and we did
not wish to sleep.

CHAPTER XIII.

A SURVEY OF THE SITUATION.

WE enjoyed our supper very much, for hunger is the best sauce. If the same meal had been set before us in the refectory of the Institute, we should have deemed ourselves a much injured body of students, because there were neither cakes nor pastry, preserves nor relishes. But the coffee made us decidedly shaky in the nerves, as I have before hinted. We had it only in the morning at the academy, and then not half so strong as our cooks made it on the present occasion.

As the darkness began to gather, some of the ingenious ones set themselves at work to provide beds for the night, and various expedients were resorted to, with no mean results. One of our blankets was big enough to cover two students, and with the other the couple made a kind of shelter tent. The dry foliage of the pine trees, which carpeted the ground in the grove, formed a soft and comfortable bed, and there was no danger that any one would suffer, unless he was too lazy to provide himself with suitable accommodations. We were used to camping out, though we were generally supplied with straw to sleep upon; but the pine foliage was a good substitute.

By the time we had finished our suppers we were satisfied that Tommy's forces must be aware .of our presence in the vicinity. Briscoe had stationed a couple of our fellows near the ravine, where they could see all that transpired on High Bluff, with orders to report any unusual movement on the part of the enemy — for as such we now regarded the major's forces, at least in a technical sense, though I am sure there was no real hatred between the parties. We were contending very much as we would have played a game of base ball, or football.

After supper Briscoe and I walked over to the sentinels' post. A group on the other side were attentively surveying the ground in the vicinity of our camp. They did not speak so that we could hear them, but we were satisfied that they had discovered us. They seemed to be much annoyed and disturbed at the fact that we had halted so near them without making any demonstration to apprise them of our presence. Probably they suspected that we were up to some trick, and intended secretly, in the sombre shades of midnight, to assault their fortress, and carry it by storm.

"As they seem to be expecting something, I think we had better stir them up a little," said the senior captain, in a low voice.

"How stir them up?"

"Why, make a feint at some point where we don't intend to do anything — just for the fun of the thing," laughed my companion.

"If we could only get over there, we could capture their camp in about two minutes and three quarters."

"I don't know about that. Sixty-five fellows, with guns and bayonets, would be more than a match for eighty-five without anything," replied Briscoe.

"The bayonet don't amount to much, nor the guns either, without powder and ball. A long pole, in our kind of warfare, is just as good as a fixed bayonet. I saw a pile of hoop-poles on the road, half a mile back. We could arm ourselves with them, and be just as formidable as though we had bayonets."

"But Tommy got a little ahead of us when he took away our muskets."

"That's so; and I feel just a little cheap about it, though it was no great achievement on his part."

"Still I should like to get even with him on this point."

"So should I."

"We ought to have gumption enough to get over a chasm thirty feet wide," added Briscoe, rubbing his head to stimulate his ideas.

"We could get over easily enough if we only had the material to work with. I don't think the gully is so wide over by the road."

"Perhaps not; but what could we do if it were not more than twenty, or even ten, feet wide?" asked the senior captain, anxiously; for he was ripe for any undertaking that would give us even a temporary advantage, or enable us to obtain our guns.

"Let us find a narrow place in the gully first; then we will see what can be done."

We left the spot, and examined the gully nearly to the lake on the upper side of High Bluff. The narrowest place was at the side of the road where Tommy's party had removed the bridge; but even here it was over twenty feet wide. However, it was not more than fifteen feet deep, the waters of the stream falling into the lake over a series of cascades. It was a noisy torrent in the gully, though there were plenty of rocks above the water to afford us a standing place if we could descend into the abyss. This was the most hopeful point for operations, and a suggestion of a plan by which the difficulty might be overcome dawned upon my mind; but, as we had nothing to work with, I did not mention the idea to my companion.

We continued our walk to the lake above the bluff. Just above the inlet we found an inclined plane in the rocks leading down to the lake. Though nature had prepared the way for this descent, the hotel-keeper at Priam had done most of the work; for off the point of which High Bluff formed the extremity were the best fishing grounds on the lake. At the foot of the inclined plane, moored off in the lake, was a kind of raft, such as that upon which my friend Wolf had picked up Colonel Wimpleton, for the convenience of the fishermen. It was reached by a plank, about twenty-five feet long, covered with ledges to prevent the person who went down upon it from slipping.

"Here is just what we want," I suggested, as Briscoe and I walked down the plank to the raft.

"What?"

"This plank."

"To cross the ravine?"

"Yes."

"Good!"

"We can cross that ravine just as easily as though it were not more than two feet wide," I added, with enthusiasm; for I was quite anxious to make a reputation as an engineer, for that was the foundation of my great regard for my friend Wolf.

"I don't see it!" laughed Briscoe. "You can get this plank up to the gully; but it will be another thing to put it across the chasm. Let me tell you, this is a pretty heavy piece of lumber."

"I know that."

"If you mean to stand it up on one end, and then

let it fall across the gully, I want to tell you, in the beginning, that not enough of our fellows can take hold of it to raise it to a perpendicular," said Briscoe, anticipating a difficulty.

"I don't intend to do it in that way," I answered, rather smartly, for I was not pleased to have my new-fledged engineering skill disputed. "If you will leave the matter to me, I will give you my bond, in the penal sum of two cents, to put this plank across the bridge as soon as it is dark enough to cover the operation."

"I appoint you engineer-in-chief of the army of the rebels," replied Briscoe, with his usual good-nature. "But how are you going to do the job?"

"I have no doubt you will trump up plenty of objections to the method if I state it; therefore I would rather not do so."

"Just as you please, Skotchley."

"Don't be offended. Of course I will tell you if you desire it."

"No; I don't care."

"I will take the responsibility of the job."

"All right."

"But I want about a dozen of the stoutest of our fellows."

"You shall have the whole crowd."

"I don't want them. They would be in my way."

"But you will permit me to ask whether you think Tommy's fellows will let you cross your bridge after you have laid it down," continued Briscoe. "You must remember that the regular army, with guns and bayonets, is on one side, while you are on the other."

"If I understand your purpose, all you wish to do to-night is to obtain our guns."

"That's all. When we go over to the election we will use the tree which Jed will fell for us. But while we are about it, and you have your bridge across the chasm, why not capture the bluff?"

"That would spoil all the fun. We want to step in about the time Tommy is holding the election, and cast our votes for a good and true man for major."

"Precisely so; but if Jed should not come, or his plan should not work —"

"Hold on, Briscoe!"

"What's the matter now?" demanded Briscoe, startled by my enthusiasm as a new idea took possession of me.

"We must regulate this matter a little."

"How?"

"On the whole, I think it will be better to have the election come off in legal earnest."

"Why don't you say what you mean, Skotchley!" added the senior captain, impatient with me, as my ideas so far outreached my speech.

"I will. We must give Tommy men enough to let him have a quorum. We will pick out ten good fellows, true-blue, and send them over to-night — let them walk the plank. Of course they are not to vote for Tommy for major."

"They can if they like," added Briscoe, modestly.

"They will not. To-morrow noon, when the balloting has commenced, the rest of us will go over on the tree, and see that the election goes as it should.

"Suppose the tree should not work to suit us?" suggested the prudent senior captain.

"Then we can throw this plank over again. But

there will be no trouble about the tree — not a bit.”

“All right; I am satisfied.”

“I want you to make a demonstration, Briscoe, while we are laying down the plank.”

“I’m ready; what shall it be?”

“Anything you like.”

“As you are engineer, you must say what you will have done.”

“You can take this raft and work it over to the bluff, for I shall want one of the ropes with which it is moored, and make a feint of scaling the rocks. This will bring all of Tommy’s fellows to the spot, and I shall be permitted to work without interruption.”

“Well, I will do so. It is not necessary for me to remind you that this raft and this plank do not belong to us.”

“We will leave everything just as we find it, and make it all right with the hotel-keeper when we get to Priam.”

“I don’t like to meddle with private property.”

“Nor I; but it is one of the necessities of war.”

"Humph! Well, we will pay the damage, and recommend the hotel to all our friends. Mine host will be satisfied, I know."

Having thus disposed of this difficult question, we walked back to the camp.

10

CHAPTER XIV.

SERGEANT HACKER'S VISIT.

THE foliage was so dense in the vicinity of High Bluff that we could, for the most part, perform our operations without being seen. By the time we reached the camp, on our return, it was dark; but it was a bright, starlight evening, so that we could prosecute our enterprise without difficulty. A blast of Fryes's bugle gathered our fellows together in the road, whither they eagerly rushed, anxious to ascertain what was to be done.

It required a full hour to explain our plans and purposes to all the fellows, who were more inquisitive than Briscoe. All of them were ready to engage in the enterprise, and I was more afraid their enthusiasm would overdo the matter than that the want of zeal would defeat it. The ten who were to help out Tommy in obtaining a quorum were carefully selected.

None of them had ever been noisy partisans against the major, and would not excite suspicion when they appeared at High Bluff, but would readily be regarded as willing converts to Toppletonianism.

The party who were to assist me were also detailed, and, in company with them, I went back to the pile of hoop-poles we had seen, and obtained a supply of these sticks — not so much for weapons as for working tools. Briscoe, who was to make the feint with the rest of the force, waited my return in the vicinity of the bridge, his fellows amusing themselves in the mean time to suit their own fancy. As my party approached the bridge, Corporal Dunbold met me, with a message from my senior.

"Captain Briscoe says you are to lie low for a little while," said he.

"What's the matter now?"

"I don't exactly know; but some of the fellows say there is a spy among us from the other side."

"How did he get across the gully?"

"I don't know. Captain Briscoe says you will keep your fellows out of sight, and join him at the bridge. I will show you where he is."

I halted my party, and, telling them to remain where they were until my return, I followed the corporal, much wondering what this new phase of the situation signified. I found Briscoe seated on a rock beyond the bridge.

"What's up?" I inquired.

"Sergeant Hacker has come over to pay us a visit."

"How did he get over?"

"That's a mystery to me. Probably Haven, who is more familiar with this region than any of the rest of us, knew of a way to cross the gully before he pulled down the bridge," replied Briscoe.

"What is he after?"

"Converts, I suppose."

"Well, we have some for him. Where is he now?"

"He is holding a confab with two or three of our fellows at the side of the road. I thought of capturing him as a spy; but I think now that he will help us out with the little plan we matured," laughed Briscoe. "He was skulking about here some time before I knew he was among us."

"Perhaps he has discovered what we are about," I suggested, with some alarm.

"No; he isn't any wiser than the law allows. As soon as I made him out, I stopped everything, and cautioned the fellows not to open their mouths about anything we are doing."

"What does he say?"

"He hasn't said anything to me. I understand he asked a few of the fellows if they did not want some supper. A minute or two before you joined me I contrived to have Bowles, who, you know, is one of the ten who are to help Tommy make up a quorum to-morrow, fall in his way. They walked down the road together, and I suppose Bowles will make some kind of a trade with him."

"Are you sure Bowles is all right?"

"Of course I am."

"Suppose Hacker should offer him a commission, as an agent of the major."

"Let him offer it! I know Bowles well enough."

I was not much afraid of him myself; but I was extremely anxious to know what Hacker had to say. The conference was in progress only a few rods from the spot where I was. I left the road, and creeping softly on the pine furze which strewed the ground where our camp was located, I obtained a position near the spy and his presumed victim. The roar of the brook, as it tumbled over the rocks, favored my movement, and enabled me to secure my position without discovery.

Sergeant Hacker, in the truest sense of the word, was a partisan of Tommy Toppleton. He was looking out for himself, and being a tolerably good soldier, he doubtless expected to be chosen a lieutenant, if not a captain, in the approaching election, so that while working for the major he was really working for himself; and this is generally the character of violent partisans. On the other hand, Bowles was not a partisan, though he was a shrewd and trustworthy fellow. The conference appeared to have just begun, for I suppose there was an introduction through which the main topic had to be reached.

"But are you not hungry?" asked the messenger from the other side.

"No, not very," replied Bowles, with his usual coolness. "We had a good dinner at the farm-house after we had put out the fire."

"But you will be hungry in the morning, if you are not to-night," suggested Hacker, who seemed determined to make the question of rations the chief one.

"Very likely we shall be."

"What are you going to do?"

"Well, we leave all that to Briscoe, who is our commander now."

"Do you expect to find anything to eat in this place in the woods?"

"We may go over to High Bluff, and help ourselves out of the common stock. I take it we own a share of it."

"You can't get over."

"Perhaps we can. How did you get over, Hacker?"

"I have a way."

"We may find a way."

"I think not. The bridge is taken up, and you might as well try to jump across the lake as over that gully."

"What did you come over for, Hacker? What are you driving at? You needn't beat about the bush any longer," interposed Bowles.

"O, I only came over to see how you were getting along."

"You didn't come for that. You want something. Why don't you say what it is?"

"I didn't know but some of the fellows might want to go over to the bluff, where they could get something to eat, and have a chance in the tents. But, if they do not, I will go back again."

"I would like to go over, for one," replied Bowles, promptly.

"All right; come along."

"I'm ready."

"But are there not some other fellows who would like to go?"

"Very likely there are. How many do you want?"

"O, ten or a dozen," added the messenger, with seeming indifference. "By the way, Bowles, you know the election of officers was postponed till to-morrow noon."

"So it was, now I think of it."

"Bowles, I always liked you, and so did Tommy Toppleton. If you want to be a sergeant, you can have the place."

"Thank you. I shouldn't mind being a sergeant. In fact, I should rather like it."

"Our fellows would like to appoint you."

"Well, I will give them a chance to do so."

"But you know some of the fellows are trying to run Tommy out," added Hacker, in a low tone.

"I have heard something of that sort," continued Bowles; and certainly no one could accuse him of ever seeming to care anything about the matter.

"There are some good fellows over here, and we don't like to have them lying on the ground without any tents, and with nothing to eat. If you have a mind to pick out ten or a dozen of them, I will get them over to High Bluff."

"I will do so."

"I don't know but we can make you a second lieutenant, if you will."

"Well, that is worth trying for."

"If those fellows mean to stick to Briscoe, Tommy is willing they should. He intends to leave them out in the cold. When they are willing to come back to their duty, and obey all orders, he will let them up; but the officers who mutinied are to be punished."

"How punished?"

"Reduced to the ranks, at least," said the sergeant, with energy. "All who are willing to come back now will be received. Tommy can have it all his own way."

"I am ready to go over, for one."

"Well, who are the others?"

"There's the trouble. I have no chance to talk with them to-night."

This seemed to be the difficulty, and it was discussed for some time. Hacker proposed several plans, all of which were rejected by Bowles, who at last promised to meet the sergeant near the gully in half an hour, after he had sounded some of our party. Certainly our representative managed his case very well, and I was entirely satisfied with him. He left the spot, and walked back towards Briscoe. I rushed forward in the opposite direction, and reached the road so as to be between Hacker and his objective point, for I was desirous of speaking with him.

"Who goes there?" I called, as the messenger ap-proached.

"Sergeant Hacker," replied the spy. "Captain Skotchley, I believe. I have been looking for an officer."

"What are you doing here?"

"Flag of truce," he replied, exhibiting his white handkerchief. "I have a message from Major Top-pleton."

"Deliver it."

"He desires to say that any of the mutineers will be admitted to the camp, and may return to their duty, excepting only the commissioned officers, upon their promise to obey all orders."

"That's very kind of him. Pray, what is to become of the officers?"

"The captains will be court-martialed."

"Tell him we will all be over there to-morrow, and ask him to have his court-martial ready," I re-plied, rather disgusted with the proffered terms.

"You will not go over without the major's per-mission," retorted Hacker.

"Perhaps not."

"You forget that we have all the arms; and I think we can protect our camp from intrusion."

"If that's all you have to say, you can return."

"Major Toppleton does not wish to be responsible for your uncomfortable position here, without food or tents."

"He needn't trouble himself."

"You can deliver his message to your men. If you choose to submit, and promise to obey orders, he is ready to receive you back."

"We are not quite ready," I answered.

"Very well; the consequences are with you then," replied Hacker, moving towards the bluff.

I permitted him to depart in peace, so as not to disturb Bowles's plan, whatever it might be, though I was disposed to arrest him as a spy upon our ground. Joining Briscoe at the bridge, I found him conferring with Bowles in regard to the filling up of Tommy's quorum.

CHAPTER XV.

A STRATEGIC MOVEMENT.

"SHALL the balance of Tommy's quorum go over to-night, or to-morrow? That's the question," said Briscoe, as I joined him at the bridge.

"I don't want to go to-night," added Bowles.

"Why not?"

"I want to see the fun."

"You can see just as well from the other side of the chasm," I suggested. "Besides, you may be able to serve us better there than here."

"What can I do?" asked Bowles. "If I can be of any use over there to our party, I am willing to go."

"You can," said Briscoe. "We only intend to obtain our arms to-night — that's all. We desire to have the election go on just as though the whole crowd were there. We intend to be present at the right time. You know where we are going to operate, and you must serve us on the bluff, as you see opportunity to do so, only don't be too zealous."

" I'll go, and do the best I can," replied Bowles.

He called up the nine who were to go with him, and planned the matter to suit himself. Conducting them towards the chasm, he was soon joined by Hacker, and all of them disappeared in the woods. I was very curious to know how the party was to be transferred to High Bluff; but I was soon satisfied that it was not by crossing the gully. Briscoe and I had agreed to keep the rest of our fellows back, for Bowles had gone off with great pretensions to secrecy, as though he were veritably deserting with his followers. I crept over to the rocks near the fishing raft, and soon discovered that the party were there. They were in the act of embarking in a large boat, which, I concluded, belonged to the raft, and was the property of the hotel-keeper. They pushed off, and disappeared in the darkness. It was evident, therefore, that there was some way of reaching the summit of the bluff from the lake side.

The coast was clear now, and our fellows were silently led to the raft by Briscoe. Those who were to assist me pulled up the plank, and, having secured one of the ropes with which the raft was moored, we carried it to the road near the point where the bridge had been removed.

" Now we want to know whether there are any sentinels on this side of the bluff," said I to Sergeant Langdon.

" I don't see any."

" Go to the chasm, and make a slight noise. If there is any one there, it will start him up."

Langdon soon reported that he could discover no one. I had not seen any guard in this direction since dark. Tommy was doubtless satisfied that a chasm twenty-four feet wide, with perpendicular sides, could not be passed by any of our party. It had been arranged between Briscoe and myself that his party should make noise enough to engage the attention of all on the bluff, while mine were bridging the gully. As I was attaching the rope to one end of the plank, I heard the shouts of our co-laborers beyond the promontory. They had pushed the raft into position beneath the bluff, and now waked the echoes of the night with their yells.

The alarm was promptly given in the camp. We saw the garrison rush to the place where the arms were stacked, and we lay low until they had left for the point of danger. There was evidently a great deal of excitement among Tommy's adherents. Perhaps they expected a violent assault upon their works.

"Now, lively, fellows!" I called to my party, as they picked up the plank and bore it to the chasm.

The end to which I had fastened the rope was dropped into the abyss, so that it rested upon a rock which I had before selected. With a couple of the hoop-poles we pushed the upper end over to the other side of the gully, where it was to rest as part of the bridge. By the rope attached to the lower end we pulled it up, and placed it on the rock. The experiment was a complete success, and I was very well pleased with my first attempt at engineering. It was a very simple experiment, after all; and though satisfied, I was not vain of the result.

I was the first to cross the plank; but my fellows all followed me. Taking six or seven muskets apiece, we soon placed them on the right side of the gully, and our work was accomplished. Briscoe's forces were still shouting as though their salvation depended upon the amount of noise they could make. If there were any night voyagers on the lake in that vicinity, they must have suspected that the demons of this wild region were engaged in an hilarious frolic; but I think there was no one within hearing of our voices.

"I say, captain, we might as well finish the job, now we are here," said Langdon, after we had stacked the arms by the side of the road.

"How finish it?"

"Wouldn't it be better to have the bridge material on this side of the gully?" suggested the sergeant.

"I don't know that it would."

"We could hold Tommy and his party as prisoners then."

"Possibly it would be a good move; but when we go over to-morrow, we must do it with a rush, after the balloting has begun."

We decided to transfer the bridge materials to our side of the chasm. Perhaps it was just as well, so far as Tommy was concerned; for I did not believe, after I had looked at the heavy timbers which comprised the string-pieces, that he had the engineering skill to reconstruct the bridge. We completed our work in a very short time, and without any interruption from the valiant garrison which defended the place. Having finished the job, we placed the plank on six sticks, and with one boy at each·end of them, conveyed it back to the lake as we had brought it up. Briscoe's party were still demonstrating under the high cliff of the island. Langdon, who could whistle like a locomotive through his fingers, made the signal we had agreed upon that our work was finished.

By this time most of us were thoroughly fatigued, and I felt that a bed of pine furze in the grove would be as good as a downy couch for me. We had worked off the effects of the potations of strong coffee, and some of us were so sleepy that we could hardly keep our eyes open. One of the cooks lighted a match, so that I could see the face of my watch, and I found that it was almost midnight. But we had to wait nearly an hour before Briscoe's fellows could work the raft back, for it was a clumsy thing to handle in deep water. When they came in sight, they were towing it with the large boat in which Hacker had conveyed his recruits to the fortress. Without it I doubt whether they could ever have brought the raft back to its moorings. We were too tired to put the raft in position as we had found it, and, making it fast to the shore, returned to our camp.

We were a sorry set when we turned in at about one o'clock that night; and if we had taken a vote on the question, I think we should have decided unanimously that campaigning after dark, and especially after midnight, was anything but fun. The weather was so warm that we did not need fires; and, wrapping our blankets around us, we lay down without troubling ourselves to post a single sentinel to watch over the camp while we slumbered. There was no danger of an assault from Tommy's forces, for we had them bottled up in their strong fortress. Briscoe's party had brought away the boat in which Sergeant Hacker had made his visit to our camp, and there was now no possible way for any of the enemy to reach us.

The garrison on High Bluff were as much fatigued as we were, and were as little disposed to make an assault as we were to repel one. I cannot speak for others, except to say that no one disturbed us; and I slept like a rock upon my hard bed. It was after eight in the morning when I waked; but not a single soul seemed to be stirring. I was in no hurry; so I turned over and went to sleep again, as all my companions were still slumbering.

"Hallo, Skotchley!"

I opened my eyes. It was Briscoe.

"We are sleeping all day," said he.

"What's the odds? We have nothing to do but eat breakfast until noon. We may as well rest ourselves while we have the chance."

"But it is after nine o'clock," laughed he.

"I think I have slept enough, then," I replied

springing to my feet, well satisfied that no rheumatism had found a lurking-place in any of my joints.

Some of the fellows were already up, and among them Fryes, who was directed to blow a blast on his bugle to wake the slumberers. In a few minutes we had them all on their feet. I went to the rushing brook, and took an eye-opener in the shape of a splendid wash in the clear, cold waters, which made me feel like a new man, fit for the great enterprise of the day. Frying bacon without a frying-pan was declared by the cooks to be a difficult achievement; but an iron kettle was a tolerable substitute. We boiled half a bushel of potatoes, and by ten o'clock we were ready for our morning meal. As an expedient for plates, we used smooth, flat stones, taken from a slate ledge a few rods from the camp. The breakfast was eminently satisfactory.

"Where is Jed?" asked Briscoe, as we rose from the ground when the repast was finished. "He has not come yet."

"I think he will come," I replied.

"Suppose he should not come?" suggested the senior captain.

"Then we must get along without him."

"I don't see how we can."

"My party took the precaution last night to bring the bridge materials over to this side of the gully. we can put the bridge up when we want it, though it will take some time to do the job."

Briscoe laughed heartily as I explained to him that Major Tommy and his forces were actually prisoners on High Bluff, and would have to stay there until we permitted them to leave. As we intended to turn the tables upon our gallant commander-in-chief, I hoped that our precautions would not prove to be useless. It was possible that Jed might not be able to come, however good his intentions might be; and I walked down to the place where we had stored the bridge stuff, accompanied by my working party, in order to make preparations for crossing at this point if Jed should fail us. I simply fixed upon a plan for doing the work; and, after examination, I was satisfied that the method by which we had laid down the plank the night before was the best one. I then went with Briscoe's party to the

fishing raft, where, in a few moments, we put everything just as we had found it.

While we were thus engaged, Jed arrived, and
we all hastened to the camp to complete the grand
coup de main of the day.

CHAPTER XVI.

THE PINE TREE BRIDGE.

JED had arrived with his sharp axe. He had also brought with him a bill-hook, to clear away the underbrush on the verge of the chasm, so that it need not impede our movements when the decisive moment arrived. Jed and one of the large fellows soon cut the bushes down, but we did not remove them. They were piled up so as to form a screen to hide the operations on our side from the view of those on the bluff. They were so arranged that the fall of the pine tree would tumble them into the abyss, and leave everything clear, so that we could rush over before the enemy could gather on the other side to oppose our passage.

The occupants of High Bluff did not seem to be in the best of spirits. They had doubtless discovered the loss of our share of the muskets, and of the bridge materials. The boat by which Hacker had left the bluff was no longer available, and they could not help understanding that they were prisoners. In fact the tables were already turned. But we were confident that the election would not be neglected. If Major Tommy was convinced that his command were prisoners, he was equally well assured that our party could not disturb him without first laying down the bridge. - Probably he thought it easy enough to prevent us from putting the timbers across the gully, as, indeed, it was.

Jed was already at work on the pine tree. It was exceedingly important to prevent the garrison on the bluff from knowing what was going on at this point; but the sound of the woodman's axe in that locality was not a strange one. It need excite no suspicion. But we saw several of Tommy's adherents making a critical examination to ascertain what our party were doing. The bushes effectually concealed the work from their gaze.

"Come, Skotchley, we must not take it too easily," said Briscoe. "If those fellows should snuff what we are doing, they might spoil everything. You must make a demonstration where the bridge was."

"I intended to do that at the right time," I replied, looking at my watch. "It is about time now — half past eleven."

"You are the engineer, captain. What do you intend to do?"

"I am going to commence laying that bridge just before twelve o'clock. I want about half the fellows. The other half will stand by the tree, and go over as soon as it falls. When they have crossed, we will all rush up and join you on the other side."

"Jed has cut the tree more than half through, **and** a few clips on the other side will drop it."

"All right."

I took half the force, and marched down to the road. Half a dozen sentinels guarded the bluff on the other side at this point. It was evident that Tommy and Haven did not expect an attempt would be made to cross the chasm at any other place. I did not wonder at their conclusion, for it seemed quite impracticable for a party of boys to span the arm of the lake, where it varied from thirty to a hundred feet in width. Our entire force had taken their muskets, and so far we now stood upon an equality. Each could oppose bayonet to bayonet.

I halted my detail on the verge of the gully where the bridge had been removed. As soon as we appeared, Haven marched his portion of Company A down to the threatened quarter, and halted on the other side. I was not quite satisfied with this movement, for I wished Tommy to send his whole force to oppose my operation. I walked up to the edge of the chasm, and looked into it.

"What are you going to do now?" shouted Haven.

"You shall see pretty soon," I replied, good-naturedly.

"Do you think of coming over here?"

"Well, I had thought of it."

"All right. The major has informed you in regard to the terms upon which you can return to your duty — a general amnesty to all except commissioned officers."

"He is very generous."

"I think that he is fair. We are going to have the

election over here at twelve o'clock precisely," continued Haven, in taunting tones.

"I'm glad to hear it."

"But are you not coming over to vote?"

"Perhaps we shall."

"I guess not — unless you should come under arrest," replied Haven, glancing into the ravine which yawned between us.

"Probably we shall be over to help you vote."

"I don't see it."

"You forget that we have the bridge stuff on this side."

"I should like to see you lay it down!"

"Should you?   I don't believe you are quite sincere, Haven.   But we shall have a bridge in season to vote."

"You must be in a hurry, then."

"Then I think I won't stop to talk any longer."

"I think you had better not waste any more time, if you are coming over to vote.   The polls will be closed at twenty minutes past twelve."

"I suppose I can vote if I go over."

"O, certainly!"

I directed a dozen of my working party to bring one of the string-pieces of the bridge to the chasm. We had secured the ropes with which the bridge had been removed, and I deliberately tied one end of it to the timber. The party on the other side watched my movements with intense interest. It was plain that Haven was not quite satisfied, and by no means as confident as he pretended to be. He knew that we had crossed the chasm in the night, and perhaps gave us credit for more skill than we actually possessed. I was pleased to see him send a messenger to the rear of his position; and, in a few moments, the other company, under command of Barnscott, marched down to reënforce him. At the same time Major Tommy appeared upon the ground. The little magnate consulted a few moments with Haven, and then retired. He seemed to be absorbed in another matter, which I concluded was the balloting for officers.

I could hardly conceal my satisfaction when I saw that the idlers in the vicinity of the pine tree had all been called away. Indeed, there was nothing to attract their attention at this time, for Jed had ceased chopping after he had prepared the tree on one side.

I afterwards ascertained that none of Tommy's party suspected the movement in the direction where it was really in progress. It was easier for them to believe that some farmer had come into the woods to get out a stick of timber for a special use than that our fellows intended to cross the gully in any such manner.

I ordered my party to drop one end of the string-piece into the chasm. I was promptly obeyed. This movement created great excitement on the other side. Haven rallied his force in readiness to prevent the stick from being landed on his territory.

"Out of the way, on the other side!" I shouted. "If this string-piece should hit you on the head, it might hurt you."

"Let it come!" replied Haven. "We will take care of it."

With the aid of the poles, we threw the upper end of the stick over to the other side of the chasm. The instant it touched the edge, Haven and his men tumbled it down into the abyss, precisely as I supposed he would do.

"Hurrah! Hurrah! Hurrah!" shouted the adherents of Tommy Toppleton, satisfied that they had gained a decided victory.

"Throw us another of them!" called Haven, derisively.

"Don't cry yet!" I replied. "We will have a bridge over in season to vote."

"Over with it. I think we can throw the timbers down as fast as you can set them up."

"Man the rope here, fellows!" I shouted to my party. "Work as though you were in real earnest! Heave ahead!"

Slowly, and with great difficulty, the end of the timber was pulled out of the chasm, and I prepared to make a new attempt. All of Tommy's army was in front of me. The major was very busy. I saw him place a tin kettle on a rock, and station three sentinels before it. This, I soon ascertained, was the ballot-box, and the three sentinels were the committee to assort, count, and declare the vote. Bowles was one of them, and this fact did something to assure me that fair play would be had. It was our custom to vote for each officer on a separate ballot; and, of course, the first was for major. Tommy came down to the front, and announced that the polls were open.

"Bring in your ballot for major for the ensuing year!" shouted Haven, looking over to our side, as though the remark was addressed to us. "We can vote and fight at the same time."

"All right! We are going right over," I replied, as they tumbled the end of the timber into the gully a second time.

"The polls will be closed if you wait to lay this bridge," retorted Haven, in excellent humor.

"You attend to your voting, and we will take care of the bridge."

I again heard the vigorous blows of Jed's axe, and I expected every moment to see the pine tree fall across the gulf. Our party were very much excited, and we worked at the timber with the most deceptive zeal. We threw it over upon the other side, as we had done before.

"Stand by here!" shouted Haven. "Tumble it down, quick!"

And down it went into the gully. The party on

The Pine Tree Bridge.   Page 177.

the other side gave three more rousing cheers, to celebrate the third repulse of the stick.

"Why don't you throw up your bridge!" screamed Haven, almost beside himself with excitement.

"Keep cool over there," I replied, as calmly as I could. "There is no such word as fail."

"I think there is — three such words! And there will be another when you throw that timber over again."

"Try again! That's our motto," I answered, glancing at the top of the tall pine, which was tottering and ready to fall.

It shook a moment, and then came down with a heavy crash. Briscoe, with his drawn sword in his hand, was the first to cross the abyss. He was closely followed by the rest of his party. Before Tommy and his adherents could fairly understand what the matter was, our senior captain had formed his men in line, and presented a wall of bayonets to cover the advance of my party.

"There's our bridge!" I cried to Haven, as I ordered my men to take their guns and hasten to the pine tree.

We followed Briscoc's lead, and in a few moments our entire force was on High Bluff.

"Now give them three cheers, Briscoe, in answer to theirs," I suggested; and they were given with a zeal becoming the victory we had won.

CHAPTER XVII.

THE FIRST BALLOT.

TOMMY and his forces on High Bluff seemed to be paralyzed by the sudden and unexpected movement initiated by Briscoe, and followed up by my party. They did not pay much attention to voting just then, though quite a number of them had deposited their ballots before the falling of the pine tree. We waited a reasonable time to be assaulted; but Major Toppleton seemed to be too much astonished to organize an attack upon the bold assailants. He stood in front of his men, consulting earnestly with Haven.

"Why don't you move on, and pitch into them?" said Jed, who had come over on the pine, with the axe in his hand.

"We are not going to pitch into them," replied Briscoe.

"We don't want any of them to escape," I added.

"Leave that to me," said Jed. "I will stand guard here, while you go up and do your voting. I can handle the whole crowd."

Our first business was to deposit our votes. We had already provided ourselves with ballots.

"Music!" said Briscoe; and Fryes started Hail, Columbia.

Breaking into column, we marched towards the tin kettle, which constituted the ballot-box. This movement ended the conference between the two leaders of the other side. The major ordered his men into line. By this time Bowles's party had gathered around the voting place, as they had been instructed to do by him, in order to defend the purity of the election. It was plain that Tommy did not intend to do any fighting. It would have been very foolish for him to do anything of the kind. He marched his adherents up to the vicinity of the rock where the ballot-box was deposited, and halted. Briscoe did the same. While the latter was preparing to send his men up to vote, in small parties, Haven appeared before us.

"Major Toppleton desires to know what your

intentions are," said the messenger, in a haughty tone, which, however, indicated more of disgust at our proceedings than of pride at his own.

"We came over to vote," replied Briscoe.

"I told you we were coming over, Haven," I added.

"You told me, too, that you were going to lay that bridge; but you didn't," sneered the ambassador.

"What bridge?" I inquired, smiling.

"The bridge down by the road," snapped he.

"I beg your pardon."

"Didn't you say so?"

"Not at all; I had no more idea of laying down that bridge than I had of drying up the lake."

"What did you say so for, then?"

"I think I did not say so. I simply told you we should have a bridge in season to come over and vote. I believe the promise has been kept; at any rate, we are here, and in good time. I think you said the polls would be closed at twenty minutes past twelve."

"Major Toppleton does not propose to have the election continued, under the present circumstances," replied Haven.

"Why not, I should like to inquire?" interposed Briscoe.

"He is not going to have the election carried by force of arms."

"There is to be no force of arms. All parties can vote quietly, and the thing shall be fairly done."

"But you have come over here, and taken posses- sion."

"We have taken possession of nothing. There is the ballot-box just as Major Toppleton placed it, guarded by the committee whom he selected himself," persisted Briscoe.

"The major intends to postpone the election till it can be conducted fairly," added Haven.

"Allow me to suggest that it is not in the power of the major to postpone the election. It was deferred, by vote of the battalion, to this day and hour; and unless the battalion vote otherwise, it must take place at the present time."

"I will report what you say to him," said Haven, who could not conveniently answer the argument of the senior captain.

"If Major Toppleton desires to take a vote on the question of postponement, we are quite willing to do so," added Briscoe.

The messenger returned to the major; but, while the conference between them was in progress, I took care that the voting should go on, in order that the time might not expire before our portion of the battalion had deposited their ballots. Tommy's committee stood around the tin kettle, and compelled each voter to hold up his ticket, so as to make sure that only one vote was put in the box by a single person. They retained their muskets, and were zealous in the discharge of their duty. The nine fellows who had come over with Bowles stood behind the committee, as their leader had directed them to do, the moment the pine tree fell, in order to prevent the election from being suspended, or the ballot-box carried away by any of Tommy's adherents.

As our votes had been previously prepared, it required but a few moments for us to drop them into the tin kettle. Everything was done in an entirely orderly manner, under the supervision of the committee. I could not see the slightest chance for cheating, and I

did not believe there was any fraud on either side.
As our men voted, they resumed their places on the
slope of the hill, between the committee and the pine
tree bridge.

"Tommy's fellows are fooling away the time," said
Briscoe, anxiously.

"That is their lookout."

" Our fellows have all voted."

"Some of Tommy's have also. If a quorum of the
battalion have voted, the election will be according to
the by-laws, and we are all right."

"Go up to Tommy, and tell him, that, as he does
not choose to put the question on postponement, we
shall consider this as an election, and abide by the
result, whatever it may be."

I walked hastily to the spot where Tommy and
Haven were discussing the difficulties of the situation.
As I approached the major, I drew my sword, and
respectfully saluted him.

"I have a message from Captain Briscoe, senior
captain, in command of that portion of the battalion
which was excluded from High Bluff," I began.

"I don't recognize Captain Briscoe as in command

of any portion of the battalion," returned Tommy, with an effort to be dignified. "I have suspended him."

"Then I will speak for myself."

"I have suspended you, also."

"We are both ready to answer to any charges. I believe we are entitled.to vote, and we have done so. Our party have all deposited their ballots. As you have not chosen to take the question upon a postponement, we shall regard this as the election, and abide the result, whatever it may be. This is my message. I have delivered it, and will now retire."

"Do you think an election held under these circumstances ought to be considered valid?" demanded Tommy.

"I think the vote has been fairly taken, by a committee appointed by yourself. Our party are satisfied. We intend to have the vote counted, and the result declared."

"You mean it!" exclaimed the major, with an attempt at a sneer, which was only a partial success.

"Several of your party have not voted, though the

time fixed by you for keeping the polls open has expired."

"Suppose we do not choose to vote."

"That's your affair. A quorum has already voted, and that is enough. The moment the result is declared, we shall place ourselves under the orders of the new major, whoever he may be."

I saluted the major again, turned, and retired. We could do nothing more; so Briscoe and I walked up to the vicinity of the voting place. I suggested to the committee that it was time to close the polls.

"All that have not voted will do so at once!" shouted the chairman of the committee, loud enough to be heard all over the bluff. "Polls will close in a minute."

"Are you going to close the polls before all have voted?" demanded Tommy, rushing up to the tin kettle with his ballot in his hand.

"It was your order that the polls should be closed at twenty minutes past twelve," replied the chairman.

"This election is postponed till further orders," said the major.

"No! No! No!" yelled our party, who had marched up to the spot.

"It cannot be postponed except by vote of the battalion," I remonstrated.

"Then I will take a vote. Those in favor—"

"Stop a moment, if you please, Major Toppleton," interposed Briscoe. "There is no motion before the battalion. No question can be put except upon motion."

"Mr. Commander, I move that the election be postponed for one week," said Haven, coming to the assistance of his chief.

"Those in favor—"

"I object!" shouted Briscoe.

"I don't care if you do object," replied Tommy, angrily.

"The motion has not been seconded."

"Second the motion," shouted one of the major's adherents.

"It is moved and seconded that this election be postponed for one week," continued Tommy. "Those in favor will say, ay."

"Ay!" cried all of the major's party.

"Those opposed will say, no."

"No!" yelled the rebels, with a vim which proved that they understood the case perfectly.

"It is a vote!" added Tommy, triumphantly.

"I doubt the vote," said I, sure of the result, if we had fair play.

"The vote is doubted."

"I call for a division," said Faxon.

It had always been our custom, when a vote was doubted, to divide the house, each side marching between two tellers to be counted. The major evidently wished to escape this ceremony, but it was impossible, and the division took place. The conclusion could not be escaped; and, either by mistake or otherwise, some of Tommy's party voted with the rebels, so that the result was fifty-nine for postponing the election to ninety-one against it. Tommy repeated the statement of the vote, though it almost choked him. Without a word, he went up to the kettle, and dropped his vote into it. His example was followed by all the others who had not voted.

The committee were directed to count the votes.

They did so, and handed the result to the major, on a piece of paper. He read it, as follows:—

" Whole number of votes, ... 153
Necessary to a choice, ... 77

Thomas Toppleton, ... 68
Robert Briscoe, ... 85

Robert Briscoe is elected major."

CHAPTER XVIII.

THE SECOND BALLOT.

OUR fellows could not help giving three cheers when the major read the result of the vote. Tommy's face was red with rage and mortification. I do not know whether he expected, or even feared, the election of another in his place; but I do know that his tyrannical, and his supercilious behavior towards his equals had received its just reward. After the cheering had ceased, all parties looked to the major to ascertain how he bore his defeat.

By this time Haven rushed to his assistance, with words of consolation, if not of hope. He had made a discovery, which, in the excitement of the scene, had escaped the notice of most of us. He spoke with Tommy, took the paper from which the major had read the result of the vote, and, after examining it for a moment, spoke a few earnest words to his superior, whose face suddenly brightened.

"Officers and soldiers," the major began, after he had glanced at the paper again, "it was plain enough to me from the beginning that no fair election could be had in the midst of this excitement."

"It would have been fair enough if you had been elected," growled a fellow in our ranks.

"It is not fair, whoever is elected; and I, for one, will not submit to it."

"The vote has been declared, and Briscoe is major!" shouted Bowles, who regarded himself as in some sense the guardian of the purity of the election.

"There was cheating in the election, and I object to the result," said Haven. "There are but one hundred and fifty in the battalion, and one hundred and fifty-three votes were cast."

"Very likely there was other cheating," suggested Tommy, who perhaps really believed that he had been defeated by fraud.

"Let's have it over again," said Lennox, the first lieutenant of Company B.

"Mr. Commander!" called Faxon.

"Lieutenant Faxon," replied the major.

"I move that we proceed to a new election for major."

"Second the motion!" promptly added Lennox.

"It is moved and seconded that we proceed to a new election," said Tommy. "Are you ready for the question?"

Haven proceeded to make a speech, in which he attempted to show why it would be better to defer the election. Faxon, who was a ready debater, controverted the argument. Several spoke on each side; but finally the question was put, doubted, a count taken, and the postponement refused by "a strict party vote," which indicated a majority of twenty for the opposition. Again Tommy consulted Haven and several of his principal supporters. It must have been evident to him that he could not be elected.

"Officers and soldiers," said he, when we had waited until our patience was nearly exhausted, "I had hoped that you would consent to defer this election for a few days. It was my intention, if I had been elected, to resign in a short time."

"What a fib!" growled one of our men.

"We have accepted an invitation to drill with the Wimpletonians for a prize. We are in no condition to do so now, with the battalion in a state of mutiny.

If you will postpone the election till next Monday, I will say that I shall not be a candidate."

"No! No!" shouted our fellows.

"Mr. Commander, I rise to a point of order," said Lennox.

"State your point," replied Tommy.

"Whether, the battalion having voted to proceed with the election of major, any other business is in order."

"I made a proposition to the battalion to defer the election," answered Tommy, a little ruffled.

"We have just voted not to postpone," added one of our party.

"And we have just voted to have the election now," said another.

"Mr. Commander, I move that the roster be used as a check list to insure fair play," continued Faxon.

"Second the motion."

The motion was put to vote and carried.

"Mr. Commander, I move that Lieutenants Haven and Faxon, and Sergeants Hacker and Langdon, be a committee to check the names, and to receive, sort, and count the votes," said Lennox.

"Second the motion," added Bowles.

"It is customary for the commander to appoint committees," interposed Barnscott.

"The rules say, 'unless otherwise ordered,'" replied Lennox. "I believe my motion is in order."

"It seems to me this is a very fair thing, two on each side to check the names and superintend the voting," said Corporal Dunbold.

"The motion is not in order," replied the major. "The chair has always appointed committees of this kind."

"I appeal from the decision of the chair," promptly returned Lennox.

"An appeal from the ruling of the chair is taken," continued Tommy, vexed to find himself trammelled by the parliamentary usage, to which he had always been a fanatical adherent. "Are you ready for the question?"

"Question!"

"The question is, Shall the ruling of the chair stand as the sense of the battalion? Those in favor of sustaining the ruling of the chair will say, ay."

"Ay!"

"Those opposed, no."

"No!"

"The ayes have it, and the ruling of the chair is sustained."

"I doubt the vote," said Faxon.

The battalion was divided, and the question was decided against the chair by the opposition majority of twenty. Tommy bit his lips; but as, according to the "sense of the battalion," the motion of Lennox was in order, he was obliged to put it to vote. Of course it was carried by the usual majority. The committee were directed to take their stations by the tin kettle on the rock. The roster was brought out, and Faxon and Haven appointed to check the names, while the other members of the committee were to watch the voting. Fair play having been thus insured, the voting commenced. As there no longer appeared to be any danger of a collision between the two parties, our forces broke ranks. Then commenced the most tremendous "lobbying" and "log-rolling" that ever had been known in any of our deliberative bodies.

Tommy did not give up the battle. He and his

toadies coaxed, teased, threatened, and persuaded. Places on the Lake Shore Railroad and places in the battalion were offered to our fellows; but all of them were shrewd enough to see that the major's party was not the winning one. On the other hand, the votes already taken indicated that Briscoe was certain to be elected by a handsome majority. Boys, like men and rats, are ready to desert a sinking ship. The "lobbying" was not all on one side. In half an hour every name on the list was checked. The committee proceeded to count the votes.

The most intense excitement reigned on the bluff. Groups of officers and privates engaged in earnest discussion; and, passing near Tommy Toppleton, I was not a little surprised to hear him say that he expected to be successful. I concluded that he had lost his senses, or was merely keeping up appearances for a few moments longer. Perhaps he expected Haven, who was chairman of the committee, to change the current in his favor, or at least to discover some irregularity in the proceedings which would justify a postponement.

"The committee are ready to report," said one of

the privates; and the word passed through the camp, bringing all discussions to a sudden conclusion.

"Mr. Commander," said Haven, approaching the major with a paper in his hand.

"Lieutenant Haven," replied Tommy.

"The committee appointed to sort and count the votes have attended to that duty, and respectfully report: Whole number of votes, one hundred and fifty. Necessary to a choice, seventy-six. Thomas Toppleton has fifty-eight; Robert Briscoe ninety-two, and is elected."

The Briscoeites repeated the cheers they had given before, but with even more energy than on the former occasion. The result showed a gain of seven votes, and the cheering indicated a still larger reënforcement of the opposition from the other side. Again every eye was turned to Tommy, to ascertain whether he intended to submit to the will of the majority. Most of us expected something in the shape of a protest from Haven; but he performed his duty without comment of any kind. When the chairman of the committee reported, I was quite near the major, for I had no idea that we had reached the conclusion of the whole matter.

"What does this mean, Haven?" demanded Tommy, in a low tone, when the report had been read.

"I could only declare the vote as it was," pleaded Haven.

"But there is something wrong," protested Tommy.

"I could not find anything;" and Haven shook his head, to indicate that he had done his best for his friend, but had failed to find a flaw in the proceedings.

"What shall I do?" asked Tommy, sorely vexed at the situation.

"I don't know," answered Haven, blankly.

"I don't believe it is a fair thing. I don't understand it."

"Neither do I; but I don't see any way to get round it."

Tommy had been such a devoted adherent to parliamentary strictness, that he felt obliged to read the report of the committee, as it was given to him. Although it almost choked him to do so, he declared that Briscoe was elected major.

"I wish to add," he continued, with much embarrassment, "that I think there is something wrong somewhere. I submit to the change only under protest."

"What is the matter?" demanded some one in the crowd.

"I have tried to do everything for the good of the battalion, and I don't know of any reason why I should be treated in this manner. An officer under suspension for disobedience of orders is elected in my place. This does not look right to me, and I don't think your action will stand long."

"Briscoe! Briscoe!" shouted the boys, not pleased with Tommy's threat to have the election set aside.

In answer to the call, the new major mounted a rock, and, after he had been warmly applauded, made a short speech, thanking the battalion for the honor it had done him, and promising to discharge the duties of the office to which he had been elected to the best of his ability. We were then dismissed for dinner.

CHAPTER XIX.

HEALING THE BREACH.

JED, who had patiently kept guard at the pine tree bridge during all these exciting events, thought it was about time for him to be relieved when he saw us preparing for dinner. I went down to see him, paid him two dollars for his day's work, and invited him to dine with us. As the other officers were yet to be elected, I had no fear that any portion of the battalion — unless it was Tommy Toppleton — would think of such a thing as abandoning the field. The provisions brought from the Institute were already cooked, so that dinner was soon ready, and was quickly disposed of.

Tommy Toppleton was moody and sullen. If any one spoke to him, he answered only in monosyllables. He appeared to be considering the situation, and making up his mind what to do. No one believed that he ever had any intention of resigning if elected, or of declining the nomination if the election was postponed. I do not think that, even with the assistance of his father and the professors, he could have secured votes enough to elect him. The majority of us were so thoroughly disgusted with his tyranny, that we would have broken up the battalion rather than voted for him. We had accomplished what we had been laboring for over a year.

After dinner, in order to afford time for the students to prepare for the election of the rest of the officers, — for there were still some difficult points to be settled, — the voting was postponed for an hour. In the mean time, I took my working party, and laid down the bridge across the chasm near the road. Everything was thus restored to its former condition; and, so far as any mischief was concerned, no one would have known that High Bluff had been the camp of a turbulent battalion.

"Skotchley, I'm not sure but the worst part of the business is yet to come," said Major Briscoe, as he seated himself by my side on a rock, where I was resting after the fatigue of rebuilding the bridge.

"Why, what's the matter?" I inquired, though I knew that it would be no easy thing to reconstruct the battalion.

"Our fellows want to elect to the offices only those who have been on our side. If they do so, the battalion will still be in two pieces, when we want to unite them."

"I was afraid of that."

"It won't do. The other side say, if they are left out in the cold, they shall form a new company, and go off on their own hook."

"I suppose they had just as much right to go in for Tommy as we had to go in for you," I suggested.

"I want to give them all fair play," said Briscoe, warmly.

"Good! So do I."

"What can we do with Tommy?"

"I don't know. He is as savage as a meat-axe. There he sits on a rock, all by himself. I suppose he is brooding vengeance."

"We can be fair with him, and I'm in favor of being so. I suppose you are entitled to the second office, Skotchley."

"Never mind me. I don't care a fig for any office."

"I know you don't; but the fellows care for you. I was thinking that, if Tommy was willing, we might make him senior captain."

"Offer the place to him, by all means."

"You are generous, Skotchley. Of course you can do as you please about stepping aside for him."

"Upon my word, Briscoe, I would rather not be in the line of promotion."

"Don't talk about that. I don't think Tommy will take the place, but I would like to offer it to him."

"Do so, by all means."

"Will you and Faxon see him?"

"I will, for one."

Faxon was called, and he consented to accompany me on my mission to the late major. It was plain enough that he had not yet made up his mind what to do.

"I'm sorry you don't feel right about what has happened to-day," I began, as we halted before the little magnate.

"I feel right enough," replied he, looking up, and trying to smile. "But I don't think the fellows will make anything by what they have done."

"Something has been said about electing you senior captain."

"Senior captain!" sneered Tommy. "Do you think I would take a lower place than the one I have filled?"

"If you will take it, or any other place, we will do what we can to elect you."

"I don't want any place. I don't think I shall belong to the battalion any longer. The fellows have been mean to me, after all I have done for them. You and Briscoe stirred this thing up, Skotchley," he added, bitterly.

"I did what I thought was right."

"Did you think it was right to tip me out?"

"I did," I replied, firmly.

"That's the way my friends treat me — or those who ought to be my friends."

"The friendship can't be all on one side. To be candid, you have not treated the fellows well."

"What have I done?"

"You have been tyrannical and overbearing. You have tried to make your will law, without caring what others wanted."

"Humph! You learned that of Wolf Penniman."

"I don't want to say anything unpleasant now," I added. "If I can do anything for you, I am willing to do it."

"You can't do anything for me."

"I only wanted to say that I had no ill feelings towards you; and I don't think the rest of the fellows have."

"I should think they had. All that has been done to-day will be set aside as soon as you return to Middleport. Do you think my father will let me be insulted in this manner?"

"The fellows had a right to vote as they pleased," suggested Faxon.

"Of course they had; and they may take the consequences."

"Then there is no place in the battalion that you would like."

"No!"

Tommy's case was settled, and I reported the result to Briscoe.

"I suppose Tommy's father will be mad when he learns what has happened; but we must take our chances," replied the major. "Tommy was in the wrong, and we have switched him off. Whenever he will make a good fellow of himself, I shall be happy to resign my office in his favor."

Briscoe and myself then discussed the candidates for the other offices. Both of us desired to divide them fairly among the two parties, so as to heal all differences, and make the battalion a unit in sentiment.

"There's a difficulty in the way," said Briscoe. "We have two first lieutenants — Faxon and Haven. If we make Faxon captain of Company B, it will jump him over Haven, who is his senior. If we make Haven the captain, it will be treating one of our own fellows shabbily."

"Let me solve the difficulty for you. Make them both captains, and let me be the quartermaster," I interposed.

"O, no!"

"I insist," I added. "The place will suit me best."

"But the fellows won't consent."

"I will see to that."

After a long talk, I persuaded the major to let me have my own way. I preferred the position of quartermaster, for I had no military aspirations. It was agreed that we would run Haven for senior captain, and Faxon for junior. This was even magnanimous on the part of our side. We agreed upon Lennox and Bowles for first, and Hacker and Crampton for second lieutenants. Barnscott was set aside, for he had in turn sold out both sides, and neither party had any confidence in him. He was anxious to be a captain, and had trimmed his course to accomplish his end; and, like others who are true to nothing, he failed in everything.

We wrote tickets with these nominations upon them. They were readily accepted, and I was pleased to see that the Tommyites were entirely satisfied. The polls were opened again, and the ticket was indorsed by a large majority. Barnscott protested, engineered, log-rolled, and lobbied; but he failed to defeat the arrangement. As soon as the voting was finished, the battalion was formed in line. The shoulder-straps were exchanged to suit the new rank of the several officers. Tommy still sat on the rock, watching the proceedings. As I passed near him, he beckoned to me, and requested me to deliver his shoulder-straps to Briscoe, which I did. So far as I could see, every one was satisfied except Barnscott, who had been appointed sergeant-major. He accepted the position, but with very ill grace.

The major then made a little speech to the battalion in regard to the prize drill. His remarks were received with applause; and, when he directed the companies to separate, for the purpose of practising the manual, I was pleased to see that an excellent spirit prevailed throughout the corps. As I had no duties to perform in connection with the drill, I went over to our camp on the other side of the gully, to look after the stores there. While I was gathering them together in readiness to be loaded upon the wagons, I saw Tommy walk up the road. He did not seem to be going anywhere, for he had not taken his pony. He was apparently still brooding over his imaginary wrongs, and I wondered that he did not ride back to Middleport to report the wickedness of the battalion to his father.

While I was gathering up the stores, Jed came over on the log of the pine tree. He had witnessed the deposition of his enemy, and he appeared to be satisfied with the result. He remarked, good-naturedly, that we had "fixed that Toppleton boy," and he hoped it would be a good lesson for him. If there was nothing more he could do for us, he would go home, though he had done a good day's work, and made more than he could by staying at the farm.

Unhitching the old mare, he started for home. I heard his wagon rattling along the road for a few minutes, and then forgot all about him. I finished my work, and was about to return to the bluff by the way of the pine tree, when I was startled by a loud cry at some distance from me, down the road.

I paused and listened again. The cry was repeated, and I recognized the voice as that of Tommy Toppleton. The explanation was clear

14

enough to me in an instant.   The little magnate
had encountered Jed on the road, and the latter
was punishing him for his conduct on the preceding day.   Certainly Tommy was faring hard,
and misfortunes did not come singly to him.

CHAPTER XX.

TOMMY TOPPLETON IN TROUBLE.

I COULD hardly regard Tommy Toppleton as a friend of mine. Indeed, since the occurrences of the preceding year on the Horse Shoe, he had set himself up as my enemy. If he particularly hated any one student in the Institute, I was that one. The fact that his father and mine had been strong friends for many years did not help the matter at all. On the contrary, it made it rather worse; for the father extended to me some consideration on account of my parents, which the son resented.

More than once the little major had aimed the shafts of his malice at me; but, though I resented his open insults, I never hated him, and never attempted anything like revenge for the injuries he inflicted upon me. When I heard him cry for help, I was as willing to assist him as though he had been my best friend. Wolf and I had often talked about Tommy, and I think I had learned from him something of that spirit of true Christianity which inspires one to love his enemies.

The story of Wolf's conduct when Waddie Wimpleton was captured and threatened with a coat of tar and feathers by his enemies, had been faithfully circulated on both sides of the lake. Some of the fellows thought Wolf was a "spoony" on that eventful occasion; but, for my part, I regarded his behavior with intense admiration. To forgive and help an enemy — one's bitterest enemy — seemed to me to be a sublime thing, and I hoped I should have the grace and the courage to do likewise under the same circumstances. Acting from this inspiration, therefore, I was eager to do what I could for Tommy when I heard his outcry.

The sound came from some distance down the road, and it was evident to me that I could not reach the spot in season to do any good. But this thought did not prevent me from making the attempt, and I ran with all the speed I could command till I reached the summit of a hill, which afforded me a view of the road for a quarter of a mile. At the foot of the declivity I saw the wagon. Behind it were Tommy and Jed. The stout farmer held the little magnate by the collar. There had evidently been a struggle, from which both appeared to be resting for a moment.

"Let him alone!" I shouted, at the top of my lungs, as I hastened forward towards the scene of action.

Jed held his prisoner fast, but did not appear to be disposed to proceed to extreme measures at once. I concluded that Tommy, seeing that help was at hand, ceased his struggles to escape. At any rate, I arrived upon the ground before the conflict was resumed.

"Come, Jed, let him alone," said I, as soon as I could speak after the violent exertion I had made.

"I guess not!" replied Jed. "Not if I know myself; and I think I do."

"Pitch into him, Ned," pleaded Tommy.

"I have no quarrel with you, cap'n," added Jed. "But I'm going to take this Toppleton boy home with me, and teach him better manners."

"No, you're not!" snapped Tommy.

"You say not; but I say I am."

"Come, Jed, don't be foolish. You won't make anything by such a course as that. Let him go, and I will see that everything comes out right," I pleaded.

"See here, cap'n; you don't understand this case. When I came up to this Toppleton boy, I asked him a civil question, and he sauced me."

"'Twasn't a civil question," snarled Tommy.

"I asked you if you were ready to pay for the damage you had done to our place. Wasn't that a civil question?"

"No, it wasn't."

"Yes, it was. Then I told him not to give me any of his impudence, and he picked up a rock, and was going to heave it at me, when I jumped out of the wagon and lit on him," continued Jed, turning to me.

"I think you had better let him go, Jed," I added.

"If I do, he'll heave rocks at me."

"No, he won't."

"Perhaps I will," interposed the impracticable little magnate.

Tommy Toppleton in Trouble. Page 215.

"There, do you hear that?"

"That's only talk," I explained.

"Let me alone!" shouted Tommy, beginning a desperate struggle for his liberty.

"Let him go!" I interposed, taking Jed by the arm; for I was afraid the stout fellow would inflict some serious injury upon his puny victim.

"I'll let him go," replied Jed, shaking the little major as a terrier shakes a rat.

"Let him alone!" I repeated, earnestly, as I endeavored to stay the arm of the stalwart farmer.

Jed evidently began to regard me as an ally of his victim, and in his zeal he struck me a severe blow upon the head, which sent me reeling into the bushes by the side of the road. My senses were somewhat confused; but my ire was roused by the ungenerous blow. I looked about me for a club; but, before I could find one, I saw Jed, whose right hand was fastened upon the back of Tommy's collar, seize him by the trousers with the left hand. Lifting his victim clean from the ground, he tossed him over the end-board into the wagon, as easily as though he had been a spring lamb.

I could not find any club, and perhaps it was more fortunate for me than for Jed that I could not; for he seemed to regard me as an enemy, and was disposed to treat me as such. I picked myself up, and tried to collect my scattered senses. I had already come to the conclusion that the fist of the stout farmer was as hard as iron, for I felt as though I had been struck with a sledge-hammer. I had done all I could do; and that was nothing at all, unless I had helped to irritate Tommy's powerful assailant.

Jed held his victim down with one hand, while he jumped into the wagon himself. The little major was not inclined to yield the battle even yet, and made another ineffectual effort to release himself from the iron grasp of his captor. Tommy screamed till the wild forests were vocal with his cries; but no one but myself was within hearing of his voice. The determined farmer tossed him over upon the seat, and then took his place at the side of his conquered foe. Throwing one arm around his body, he took the reins with the other, and drove off at the best speed of the old mare.

Tommy had doubtless provoked this man beyond the limits of endurance; but I was not prepared to believe that he intended to inflict any serious injury upon him. The young gentleman had been accustomed to being "monarch of all he surveyed," and opposition from a common farmer galled him sorely. Jed had pulled him from his horse the day before, under strong provocation, and after this act Tommy could not indulge in anything like conciliation. I tried to imagine what the captor intended to do with his prize. I was willing to believe that he meant to give him a sound thrashing, and thus, to use his own language, "teach him better manners." Perhaps a little discipline of this sort would do Tommy no harm; but I could not make up my mind exactly what sort of people dwelt in the farm-house. Christy Holgate appeared to be a prisoner there; and I was not sure that the little magnate might not be subjected to something worse than a whipping.

It was useless for me to attempt to chase the wagon on foot. It had now disappeared behind a hill, and I was not disposed to follow it. I decided

that it would be better for me to state the case to
Briscoe; and, if Tommy did not soon return, an
expedition might be sent for him. I hastened back
to the camp; but, to my surprise, I found that the
battalion had marched for Priam. The stores in the
grove had been taken. I suppose I was not missed.
I had directed the wagoners to take the articles
I had piled up for them, before I left the bluff.
Glancing at my watch, I saw that the new
major had not started till the hour he had appointed for that purpose. Tommy's pony was still
on the bluff; but he was saddled ready for use.
Probably Tommy was supposed to be in the vicinity when the column moved off; and he was to
be permitted to follow, or not, according to his im-
perial pleasure.

I concluded to mount the pony, and follow the
battalion, though, as it had half an hour the start of
me, I could hardly expect to overtake it before reaching Priam, which was only three miles distant. I
was still "a little mixed" about the head, and the
puny steed was disposed to go much faster than I
was willing to let him. I overtook the column just

as it was entering Priam. The band was playing one of its choicest airs, and the people were rushing out to see the show. Urging forward the pony, I astonished Major Briscoe by presenting myself, thus mounted, at his side.

"Where's Tommy?" demanded he, looking exceedingly anxious.

"He's in trouble; and I want some help to go after him," I replied.

Briscoe halted his command, and I briefly related to him the incident of which I had been a witness.

"If I had had this pony, I should have followed and done what I could for him," I added, in conclusion.

"But Jed isn't a bad man, I judge," replied Briscoe.

"Perhaps not; but he and Tommy are terribly incensed against each other."

"What can we do?"

"I don't know that we can do anything, for probably the mischief will be done before we can get to the farm-house; but some of us ought to go after him."

" That's so."

"There comes the Ucayga!" I added, pointing to Wolf Penniman's steamer, as she was approaching the landing of the town.

It was half past six, and Captain Penniman was on time, as usual. I had an errand with the young captain, relating to the important discovery I had made at the farm-house. Major Briscoe decided to encamp for the night near Priam. I hastened down to the pier, and arrived just as the boat made fast. Leaping over the rail, I climbed to the promenade deck, where I was warmly greeted by Wolf. In as few words as possible, I told him all about Christy Holgate and Tommy. As I supposed he would, he decided to remain over until the return of the steamer from Hitaca the next morning. Colonel Wimpleton happened to be on board, and, as Van Wolter, the mate, was entirely competent to navigate the boat, the owner offered no objection to the arrangement.

We soon found the camp of the battalion;

and, after some consultation with Briscoe, I was detailed to look out for Tommy. Wolf declared that he wanted no one but me. Hiring a horse and wagon at the hotel, we departed upon our mission.

CHAPTER XXI.

CHRISTY HOLGATE.

"I CAN hardly believe the man you saw was Christy Holgate," said Wolf, as we drove off.

"I could not have been mistaken," I replied. "I knew Christy very well. I used to see him almost every day."

"But where could he have been all this time?"

"If the people at the farm-house are his friends,—as of course they are,—it was easy enough to conceal him."

"Now I think of it, I have heard Lewis Holgate say he had an aunt somewhere near Middleport. Probably this farmer's wife is Christy's sister."

"And they pretend that he is insane."

"Well, I don't know but he is. I often think a man must be crazy to commit any crime."

"What are you going to do with him, Wolf?"

I asked. "You are all alone; for I can't do much to help you."

"I am going to see if the man is Christy, first," laughed my companion.

"You may be sure of that."

"I'm going to have a talk with him, then."

"You can't arrest him yourself."

"I don't want to arrest him. If he has spent two years on this farm, confined to his chamber in the attic, I will venture to say he is not a fit person to send to the state prison. You say he looked thin and pale?"

"Very."

"If he has been confined to the house all this time, probably he has not spent my father's money."

"Don't you suppose his wife knows where he is?"

"Probably she does, and Lewis also."

"They may have spent the money for him."

"Lewis has earned good wages ever since his father left, and the two daughters work in stores. The family never appeared to have much money. Everybody supposes they live on what they earn. But we can't tell much about it."

After a drive of little more than an hour, we came in sight of the farm-house. I began to be quite nervous in view of encountering Jed and the rest of the family; but Wolf was as cool as though he were at the wheel of the Ucayga. He did not say in what manner he intended to accomplish his purpose, either in securing Christy or redeeming Tommy Toppleton from bondage. It was nearly dark when we drove up the yard, where our line had been formed to put out the fire. I glanced at the window in the attic which opened from the crazy man's room. The green paper curtain before it was suddenly dropped, and I was confident Christy was still there, though the room could not be in very good order, after the action of the fire and water. The long ladder by which we had passed up the water still rested against the house, as we had left it.

As soon as we stopped, Jed appeared, coming from the barn with a pail of milk in each hand. He instantly recognized me, and I thought he did not look very amiable.

"Don't say a word about the crazy man," said

Wolf, when I indicated to him that the man with the milk-pails was the captor of Tommy Toppleton.

"Christy is in his room; for I saw the curtain drop as we drove up," I added, in a low tone.

"All right."

"How are you again, Jed?" said I, getting out of the wagon.

"First rate!" replied he, rather gruffly.

"What have you done with Tommy Toppleton?"

"I haven't done anything with him," replied Jed, setting down his milk-pails.

"The last I saw of him, he was in your wagon, coming this way."

"Well, he didn't come far with me," answered Jed; but he seemed to be more embarrassed than the occasion required, if he was telling the truth. "As soon as he cooled off, I let him go."

"Where was that?" I inquired, astonished at this information.

"About a mile and a half this side of where you saw us. You see, he begged my pardon, and promised to settle for what mischief he had done."

"Did Tommy beg your pardon?"

"Certainly, he did."

This was the most incredible thing he had yet said.

"Tommy is not in the habit of begging any one's pardon," suggested Wolf.

"Well, he got scared, you see."

We did not see it.

"Which way did he go?" I asked.

"He went back towards the camp," answered Jed.

I was not satisfied with this story. If Tommy had been liberated at the point indicated, we should certainly have discovered him somewhere on the road. He would not have taken to the woods, but would have continued on his way to Priam, after he found that the battalion had left High Bluff. Besides, it was not reasonable that Tommy had apologized to his enemy. He had never been known to do such a thing, and, in the frame of mind in which I had last seen him, he was not likely to do so.

"We have just come down from Priam, and did not see anything of him," I added.

"I don't know anything about that. I meant to give the little rascal a sound thrashing, and teach him better manners. I know just how that boy behaves down to Middleport; how he lords it over man and boy. I used to think if ever I got hold of him, I'd lick him. Now, he insisted on scaring my colt, to say nothing of risking my life and Clarissa's; then he trod down our spring wheat, and sent his fellows through the garden; and if ever a man was mad, I was. After you put the fire out, I tried to think better of him for your sakes. If he hadn't sauced me again, I shouldn't have meddled with him. When he threw rocks at me, I meant to give him some; but he backed down, and I didn't do anything to him, to speak of."

"You wouldn't have gained anything by thrashing him," I replied. "His father would have prosecuted you."

"I don't care for that; two can play at that game, as well as one," retorted Jed, beginning to be excited.

"Well, if he isn't here, we may as well drive on," interposed Wolf, starting the horse.

Jed picked up his milk-pails, and went into the back room with them.

"But he is here," said I, getting into the wagon. "I don't believe a word of that story."

"No matter," added Wolf, coolly, as he drove out of the yard.

I was rather disgusted with my companion, to find that he intended to give up the chase so easily; but I did him injustice in my thoughts. He had not even hinted a word about Christy, and I might have known that he would not depart without seeing the robber. He turned the horse up the road in the direction of Priam.

"I see what that fellow is made of," said Wolf, when we were out of the hearing of the inmates of the house. "He is both ugly and cunning."

"He is ugly enough; but there are some good things about him. He has been very obliging to us, at least."

"Because you were arrayed against Tommy Toppleton," laughed Wolf.

"He cut down a pine tree for us, which enabled our fellows to reach High Bluff."

"So that you could pitch the major out of office," replied my friend, as he turned the horse into a by-road leading into the depths of the woods, about half a mile above the farm-house.

"What are you going to do now, Wolf?" I inquired.

"I am going to attend to the business which brought us here. I don't believe Christy stays up in that chamber all the time."

It was now almost dark, and Wolf fastened the horse to a tree. We were on the verge of what was called the wild region. Below, the country was all improved, so that the farm of Jed's father lay next to the woods. We sat down on a rock, and waited till it was quite dark, when we walked down the road towards the house.

"What are you going to do, Wolf?" I asked, nervously, in a whisper.

"I don't exactly know. Perhaps we shall have to go up that ladder, and dive into Christy's room through the window."

"You can't do that," I protested.

"Perhaps not; but we will see how the land lies.

I think we had better get over the fence, and make our way to the rear of the house. There are lights in the second story window. The people are going to bed, and everything will be quiet in a few moments."

We climbed over the fence, and sat down upon a rock, to wait until the lights were put out in the house, and the occupants had time to fall asleep.

"Hush! don't say a word," said Wolf, grasping my arm.

I neither saw nor heard anything to explain the conduct of my companion; but, having full confidence in him, I heeded his request. A moment later I heard the sound of footsteps in the road. I held my breath with interest and anxiety, awed by the manner of my companion, rather than by the fact that some one was passing in the road before me. Looking through the fence, I saw a man. There was just light enough to enable me to recognize the gray coat which I had seen upon Christy, as he passed me in the attic the day before. He walked slowly up the road towards the woods.

"Follow me," whispered Wolf, as he began to

creep along the grass between the fence and the wheat; for we were in the field where the battle had been fought the day before.

We walked in Indian style, feeling our way with our feet, like cats about to pounce upon their prey. We continued in this direction till we reached the woods, through which we could not pass without making too much noise. We could not see Christy; but he had passed into the wild region. We listened, but we could no longer hear the sound of his step. With the utmost care we climbed over the fence, which was composed of logs, so that it did not yield much beneath our weight.

"Did you see him?" whispered Wolf.

"I did; and I am sure it was Christy," I replied.

"I wonder where he is gone," added Wolf.

The road was up a gentle ascent for some distance, and straight, but we could not . see the man we sought. It was evident that he had turned into the woods. It was possible that he had taken the road where we had left our horse, or that the animal would make some noise, so as to excite his attention as he passed. We crept silently along the road till Wolf put his hand upon my shoulder and we halted.

"Hark!" whispered he.

I listened. I heard a low, murmuring voice, uttering words in the most solemn strain. They became louder and more coherent in a moment, so that we could tell what was said. It was the voice of Christy Holgate. He was praying.

CHAPTER XXII.

THE PENITENT.

I CANNOT describe the feeling of awe and solemnity with which I listened to the earnest prayer of Christy Holgate. His voice was broken with deep emotion, as he pleaded for forgiveness for his sins. I need not say that Wolf was not less affected than myself, and we both listened in respectful silence to the petition of the penitent. It has been said that if a man does not grow better, he grows worse; there is no such thing as standing still in the moral scale.

The place which Christy had chosen for his evening orisons was a little open space in the bushes. The road, as I have said before, was seldom travelled, except by pleasure parties and tourists, and at the present season of the year he was not likely to be interrupted. Wolf beckoned to me with his hand, and I followed him as he crept gently through the opening into the little natural arbor.

"O Lord, thou knowest how much I have suffered for my folly and wickedness! O, help me, and pardon me, and make me a good and true man! Forgive me, O Father in heaven, and give me that peace which I have so long sought in vain!" were the concluding sentences of Christy's prayer.

He rose from his knees, taking his hat from the ground as he did so. Turning to leave, he beheld, in the gloom, our two shadowy forms. He was startled, and uttered an exclamation of alarm. We stood perfectly still, and said nothing; for it seemed to me that nothing could be said on such an occasion.

"Who's there?" said Christy, in trembling tones.

"Christy Holgate," replied Wolf, with impressive accents, "I hope you will find the peace you seek."

"Who speaks?" demanned the penitent.

"If you have made your peace with God and man, you will be forgiven," added Wolf, solemnly.

"Who are you?"

"It does not matter who we are, at present. I came after you; and it seems to have been the will of Providence that I should find you in the attitude of prayer."

"What do you want of me?" asked Christy. "Are you an officer?"

"I am not an officer. Do you feel as though your crime had been forgiven?"

"What crime?"

"The crime for which you were praying to be forgiven."

"Do you know about it?"

"I do — all about it. You robbed your friend of twenty-four hundred dollars two years ago."

"I did — I did!" groaned the penitent.

"I asked you if you felt as though you had been forgiven. You did not answer me." `

"Sometimes I feel as though the good Father had pardoned me, and again I feel as though he had not. To-night I feel more guilty than ever. I have tried to perform my duty, but I have not had the courage to do it. Will you tell me who you are? If you are an officer of justice, I will go with you. I can suffer no more in a prison cell than I suffer here."

"Why don't you go back to Middleport, confess your error, and take the consequences?"

"Because I dare not. I cannot brand my family with infamy by voluntarily going to a prison."

"Do your family know you are here?" asked Wolf, deeply interested in the story of the unhappy man.

"My wife and my daughters do; but they dared not trust Lewis with the secret. I am very wretched, and have been from the moment I stole the money."

"What did you do with the money you stole?" inquired Wolf.

"I don't like to answer that question now. You are a stranger to me."

"I am Wolf Penniman," added my companion.

"Wolf Penniman!" exclaimed Christy, starting back, and trying to recognize in the tall young man at my side the boy who had confronted him on the locomotive at the time of the robbery. "You are not Wolf!" he added, incredulously.

"I am."

"You are taller than you were."

"I have grown a little."

"You have come to curse me for the wrong I did your father."

"No; I curse no one. I can forgive you, after hearing your prayer. I think my father can forgive you also, when he knows how penitent you are. Come out into the road."

Wolf led the way to the road, and we seated our-selves on a rock, where there was light enough to see each other's faces. The penitent, who had been a stout, hearty man two years before, was now thin and pale. He did not look like the person I used to see in the engine-room of the old steamer.

"You came after me — did you, Wolf? How did you know I was here?"

"Ned Skotchley saw you yesterday at the fire."

"Did he? Well, I saw one or two boys in the attic, but I did not know them, and I didn't think they would recognize me. But I suppose it is all for the best."

"You did not tell me what you had done with my father's money, Christy," continued Wolf.

"I will tell you. I have not dared to tell any one before, for fear my brother-in-law would find it out."

"Who is your brother-in-law?"

"Moses Trottwood. He lives in this house. I told him I had buried the money in the woods; but I told him a lie. He wanted it, and I told him I could not find the place. He is a hard man," added the cul-prit, with a heavy sigh. "He has made my wife and daughters pay three dollars a week for my board, though I have always done a man's work for him ever since I came here."

"Why didn't you leave him, then?"

"I dared not. I went to my room when any one came here, and they said I was crazy. I am almost crazy. I shall be entirely so, if I stay here much longer. I am sent to my attic room when any one is here, and I haven't spoken to a soul before to-night, except my sister, her husband and son, since I first came."

"Doesn't your wife see you?" inquired Wolf, in tones of sympathy.

"No; she has been here once or twice; but they told her I was crazy, and it wasn't safe for her to see me. I rebelled once against this tyranny; but Trottwood threatened to send for an officer. I have had to work for nothing for two years, cut off from my friends, and all the comfort I have had has been in my prayers. The money is safe, just as I took it; for I always meant to give it back to your father."

"Where is it?"

"I hid it in a box under the barn. I will give it to

you this very night. I feel that God will pardon me after I have given it back to the owner. Wolf, as true as I'm a living man, I didn't mean to keep that money when I took it. Your father and I both had been drinking a little too much. I meant to give it back to him when I first took it; but when it was fairly in my pocket, I couldn't help thinking how much good it would do me. The whiskey made your father crazy, and he pitched into me so that it made me mad, and I declared he should not have the money then. After I left the engine, I took to the swamp, and wandered about for two or three days. I then made my way to my sister's. She hid me in the attic for a week, without the knowledge of her husband and son. When they discovered me, they kept my secret; but they made me pay heavily for it. I am the servant, in fact the slave, of the family."

"You shall leave to-night, if you wish," said Wolf.

"O, I do wish to leave."

"I will engage you as second engineer on the Ucayga, if you like," replied the generous Wolf. "We need another; and I am authorized to employ one. I don't think any one will meddle with you, if my father is satisfied."

"Now, Christy, you knew Tommy Toppleton — did you not?" I interposed.

"Certainly I did, very well. He was here yesterday, with his soldiers, and behaved very badly too."

"I am sorry to say he did. Have you seen him to-day?"

Christy hesitated. After the earnest prayer we had heard him utter in the solitude of his lonely retreat, where he supposed none but He who is the fountain of mercy listened to it, I did not expect him to tell a lie.

"Have you seen Tommy to-day?" I repeated, very gently.

"I have seen him to-day," he replied, after waiting a moment. "He was brought up to the house by Jed, an hour ago, or more. Jed is a terribly vindictive young man."

"What did he do to him?" I asked, anxiously.

"I don't think he hurt him after he came to the house. His father, who is more timid than he, tried to have him let the boy go."

"What have they done with him?"

"They locked him up in the attic room opposite

mine. Tommy yelled, and kicked, and pounded the door till he appeared to be worn out with his exertions. I'm afraid it will be bad business for Jed; for Major Toppleton is a powerful man. My nephew is a bad fellow, and isn't afraid of anything in this world."

"Did Tommy submit at last?" asked Wolf.

"I suppose he did. He didn't make any more noise."

"What does Jed mean to do with him?" I inquired.

"I don't know. I should not wonder if they meant to keep him a prisoner, as they have me, until they can make some money out of the affair. They are mean enough to do anything," answered Christy.

"Did they give him any supper?"

"I don't know."

"How shall we get him?" I asked; for I was determined to release him, if we had to pull the house down, though I rather preferred not to encounter Jed to accomplish the purpose.

"I don't know how we can get him out without waking the folks. If I had the key of the room, I

16

could manage it; but I suppose Jed has it in his pocket. But I am going to get that money before I do anything else," said Christy, as he led the way around the wheat field to the rear of the barn, which he entered.

He was absent some time, during which we heard him pulling up the planks. When he returned, he handed the roll of bills to Wolf, who carefully deposited it in his pocket. The rest of our mission at the farm-house was more difficult to accomplish.

CHAPTER XXIII.

THE ATTIC CHAMBER.

PERHAPS Christy Holgate overstated his moral convictions at the time he stole the money. According to his own story, he had not intended to retain it at first, though the possession was a temptation to keep it. As nearly as I could judge, his brother-in-law had intended to secure the plunder for himself, and at the same time force the wretched criminal to bear the guilt of the crime. Trottwood had compelled him to remain at his house, in the hope of getting the money. When this hope failed him, — if it had yet failed him, — he still held on to the victim, because his services were valuable.

I had to refresh my memory with a few facts which had come to my knowledge, before I could fully believe that Christy's relatives were perfidious enough to treat him as he represented that they had. A father in New Hampshire gave his son all his property, on condition that the latter should take care of him during the remainder of his life. The ungrateful son sold the farm, went to another state, and permitted the old man to die in the poorhouse. Two similar instances were within my own knowledge, and I had no difficulty, after thinking of these things, in believing that the engineer's story was all true.

Christy was a criminal before the law, liable to be sent to the penitentiary for a long period. Even his sister might have brought herself to believe that she was doing him a favor by saving him from such a fate, on the terms she and her husband exacted. The poor man's spirits were broken; he had no power of resistance, and he suffered rather than flee from his unnatural friends. Trottwood lived but to make money. His son had no higher view of life.

The capture of Tommy Toppleton was a bold and daring outrage, when the social position and influence of his father are considered. It would have been safer to kidnap some friendless boy, but it would have been a profitless task. I was inclined to believe that the imprisonment of the little magnate in the attic of the farm-house was an afterthought, and not a scheme deliberately meditated. Probably a portion of Jed's statement was true. I had no doubt that Tommy was saucy and insulting, and even that he had thrown stones at the young farmer. It was like him to do so. Thus provoked, Jed might have carried his idea of vengeance farther than he first intended, assisted by a suggestion of making money out of the operation.

Though it would have done the little gentleman no harm to remain a prisoner, under the harsh treatment of these people, for a week or two, it was neither just nor right to permit the outrage. If I had consented to it, Wolf Penniman would not; for he knew how much pain and anxiety his absence would give to Grace Toppleton, as well as to her parents, with whom the young captain was now on tolerably friendly terms.

After Christy had given up the money, we seated ourselves in the rear of the barn, to wait until we felt sure that the people in the house were sound asleep, and to consider the means by which we were to effect the rescue of the prisoner. If the door of the chamber could be opened, we could easily get him down stairs before his jailers ascertained what we were about. Christy thought he might pick the lock, but he was afraid Jed was sleeping with one ear open on account of his prisoner.

"What kind of a door is it?" asked Wolf.

"It is a common battened door, of three quarter inch boards."

"Then it is not very strong?"

"No; I could put my shoulder through it without any trouble."

"We will do it in that way," said Wolf, quietly; and he proceeded to give the details of his plan, to which neither Christy nor myself offered any objections.

"I will go up to bed," said the penitent. "In about half an hour I will break down the door, take the boy through my room, and send him down on the ladder. When you are ready, one of you had better come up the ladder, and tap lightly on the window."

"All right."

Christy left us, and we made our way back to the

place where we had left the horse and wagon. It was necessary to have the conveyance where we could start without any delay, as soon as Tommy was at liberty. I led the horse into the road, and, heading him towards Priam, fastened him to a tree. We then walked up to the front of the farm-house, stepping so carefully as not to make any noise. Everything was quiet, and I had no doubt that the farmer and his son were both sound asleep. When the half hour had expired, as nearly as we could judge, I went up the ladder, and tapped lightly on the attic window.

A moment later I heard a crash and a scream. As I afterwards learned, the sudden assault startled Tommy, who had just fallen asleep. But he had not taken off his clothes, and Christy conducted him through his own chamber to the window, taking the precaution to lock the door behind him, so as to delay pursuit when Jed came up stairs.

"Hurry up, Tommy," said I, in a low voice, as I helped the intended victim out upon the ladder.

"O, is it you, Ned?" he replied, quivering with agitation, as he recognized my voice.

"Be careful on the ladder," I added, as he commenced the descent.

He went down with all the speed his trembling limbs would permit. I was in advance of him, and kept one eye upon him, to make sure that he did not fall. He was followed by Christy, who was also very nervous under the excitement of the moment. Before I reached the bottom of the ladder, I heard a great commotion in the house. There were hurried foot-steps within; but before the inmates had discovered what the matter was, we were all upon the ground, and hurrying towards the woods, where the horse was awaiting us.

"That was well done," said Wolf.

"It was done quickly, at any rate," replied Christy. "I suppose Jed understands, by this time, that his prisoner is gone. I locked my door, as I always do, and he will think I am still in my room."

"He will see that the door of Tommy's room is broken down," I added.

"Yes, and if he stops to think, he will see that it could not have been done from the inside, for the door opens into the room."

"No matter," said Wolf, lightly. "He may think what he pleases, now we are all safe."

Arriving at the wagon, we all got in, for fortunately there were two seats in the vehicle. Wolf took the reins, and in a moment more we were on our way to Priam. Tommy was on the back seat with me, while Christy sat in front with the captain. Thus far the little magnate had not spoken a word since he recognized me, and was conscious that he was in the hands of friends. He had been terribly frightened; for, though he was not deficient in pluck, the incidents of his night's experience had been rude enough to startle even one with the strongest nerves.

As I had seen for myself, Jed handled him very roughly; and probably he had not moderated his treatment after we parted. The mere fact that he was in the toils of his bitter and vindictive enemy was enough to shake his wonted faith in himself.

"How do you feel, Tommy?" I asked, after we had ridden a short distance.

"I don't feel very well," he replied, in a tone so subdued and broken, that it did not sound at all natural. "I am sore and lame."

"Why, what's the matter?" I inquired.

"I believe that fellow meant to kill me."

"No; I think not."

"He didn't come a great way from it, at any rate," added he; and it seemed to me that he was trying to choke down a disposition to "have a good cry."

"Did he hurt you?" I asked, fearful that he had received more injury than I had before suspected.

"How much pounding do you suppose I can stand?" he replied.

"Did he pound you?"

"Half a dozen times, besides knocking me about like a dog. He hammered me with his whip several times before he got me to the house. Every time I tried to get away, he gave me some. After he locked me up in the room, I made an effort to break the door down, and he came in, and gave it to me with a strap, till I agreed to keep still. I believe he meant to kill me."

"Not so bad as that, let us hope."

"What did he mean to do, then?" demanded Tommy, who was evidently disposed to put the worst phase upon the case. "What did he shut me up in that room for, after he had licked me till I was sore?"

"I don't know what he intended to do; but I suppose it was only to punish you for what you did yesterday."

"Do you think I did anything yesterday to deserve such savage treatment?"

"Perhaps not; but certainly it is not your fault that Jed or the girl was not killed or badly injured in that scrape," I answered, willing that he should derive all the moral benefit possible from his sufferings; but I spoke only what I believed to be the naked truth. "If Jed and the girl had been in the wagon when the colt whisked round so suddenly, I don't see what could have saved one or both of them from a broken limb or a broken neck."

"You are hard on me, Ned," replied Tommy.

"Well, I only state the facts as they are. Briscoe and I told Fryes to stop playing."

The little magnate relapsed into silence. His spirit had been broken for the first time in his life. Never before had he been conquered, or treated as his relentless persecutor had treated him. I allowed him to think the matter over for himself.

"Ned, I believe you are right," said he, at last.

"I begin to think I was in the wrong, and perhaps this fellow has given me no more than I deserve."

"His conduct was wrong; it was outrageous, whatever may be said of yours," I replied.

"Ned, I have been very miserable to-day. I was so before I met Jed in the road. I was thinking, as I walked along, what I had done to make the fellows hate me so badly."

"I don't think they hate you. They won't stand your tyranny — that's all."

"They don't like me, any how."

"That's so," I answered, candidly.

He was silent again. I was glad to learn that he had begun to review his past conduct before the ruffian took him in hand. It seemed to me that Tommy had SWITCHED OFF.

"Who is this man on the front seat?" whispered Tommy.

"Christy Holgate."

I told the story of Christy in a whisper, so that the subject of it, who was busily engaged in conversation with Wolf, should not hear me.

We had two penitents that night.

CHAPTER XXIV.

THE DISASTER ON THE WHARF.

IT was long after midnight when we arrived at the hotel in Priam. We were all fatigued enough to retire immediately, and Tommy Toppleton and I took a room together at his suggestion. He did not like to be alone, and I judged that he found it difficult to banish the image of his terrible tormentor from his mind. Without distorting the truth in regard to his past conduct, I did all I could to comfort him. When he undressed himself, I was shocked to see the bruises and wales upon his body. He had suffered much more than I supposed; but he conducted himself with much fortitude, and I really sympathized with him.

I washed the wales in cold water, and did everything for him which the circumstances permitted. He did not say much after we went to the room, except to express his gratitude to Wolf and myself for the service we had rendered him. I did not wake the next morning till the young captain rapped on my door. I admitted him and Christy Holgate.

"How do you feel, Tommy?" asked Wolf, tenderly, as my bedfellow opened his eyes.

"I don't feel very well," replied he.

"Perhaps you had better go down on the boat with me."

"Thank you, Wolf. I will. I intended to join the battalion and serve in whatever place the new major gives me, just to show that I am right towards the fellows," added Tommy, languidly; "but I don't feel able to do so."

Tommy had, indeed, switched off!

"Do you feel sick?" inquired Wolf.

"I do; and I want to go home. Before I go, I wish you all to promise me one thing."

"What is that?"

"Do not say a word to any one about what has happened to me at that house — not a word," answered Tommy, earnestly.

"Why so?" inquired Wolf.

"I'll tell you another time. I will be down stairs in a few minutes."

Our visitors retired, and I saw that my companion was suffering much pain. He was hardly able to get out of bed, and I assisted him in dressing himself.

"I don't see how we can keep this affair still, Tommy," said I. "All the fellows will want to know where you have been."

"Don't tell them. I have fought the battle, and got the worst of it. I don't want to be laughed at, and I don't want to be pitied. I feel sick, and I'm all used up."

"You will have to tell your own folks about it."

"No, I will not," he protested stoutly, even in his weakness.

"They will see the marks upon your body."

"I shall not say where I got them."

"Don't you intend to prosecute Jed for what he has done?"

"No!" he replied, decidedly. "If I can get out of this scrape, I will never get into another."

I was entirely satisfied that he should have his own

way. I helped him down stairs, for I found that he needed my assistance. He paid the bill of the whole party at the office, and ordered a wagon to convey him to the steamer. I was really alarmed about him, for though he put the best face upon his condition, I was certain that he was very ill. He was hot and feverish, and I was glad that in a couple of hours more he would be at home.

I went on board of the Ucayga with him, as she made fast to the wharf. Wolf gave him his state-room, and he lay down in the berth. I shook his hand as I left him, and he pressed mine with the warmth of a true friend. Leaving him, I went down to the engine-room, at the door of which Christy was waiting, deeply agitated in view of his approaching meeting with the man he had wronged. Wolf and I went in first, to prepare the way.

"Father, here is the money you lost two years ago — twenty-four hundred dollars," said the young captain, presenting the roll of bills to the astonished engineer.

"You don't mean so, Wolf!" exclaimed Mr. Penniman.

"Count the money, father, and see if I don't."

"Where in the world did you get it?"

"Ned, here, put me on the track of it yesterday, and that is the reason I left the boat. But, father, we haven't much time to talk now. I found Christy Holgate on his knees begging Heaven for forgiveness of his crime. If God can forgive him, surely you can, father, for Christy gave me back the money. He is a new man now."

"Well, but —"

"Here he is, father," interrupted Wolf, leading the penitent into the engine-room.

"There's my hand, Christy," said Mr. Penniman, suiting the action to the word. "What my boy says I believe."

"Ralph, I don't deserve any favors from you; but I have suffered more with this money than you have without it," replied the penitent, with deep emotion. "If God forgives me, and you forgive me, Ralph, I shall be at peace, whatever happens to me in this world."

"It's all right, so far as I am concerned," added the engineer.

"He is to be the assistant engineer of our boat,

17

father. I have given him the place. Colonel Wimpleton told me to engage one some time ago."

"All right! But do you drink anything now, Christy?" asked Mr. Penniman.

"Not a drop. I haven't tasted any kind of liquor since we drank together in the engine-room of the Ruoara."

"Nor I!" exclaimed Mr. Penniman.

"And with the grace of God, I never will again."

"Nor I!"

The bell rang to start the engine, and I rushed for the plank. It was hauled in, but I jumped ashore without difficulty.

"Look out for Tommy," I shouted to Wolf, as the boat began to gather headway.

"I will take good care of him," replied Wolf.

"Where's that crazy man?" shouted some one near me.

I turned, and saw Jed Trottwood driving his four-year-old colt down the pier.

"Where is he?" demanded he, fiercely, as he reined in his fiery animal.

"On board that steamer," I replied.

"Stop her! Stop her!" yelled Jed, at the top of his lungs. "Here, hold my colt!"

The colt certainly needed holding; for, as the steamer began to tumble the volumes of water out behind her, he became alarmed, and stood up, as he had done when we first saw him. The driver, who was not so cool as when Miss Clarissa was at his side, tried to get out of the vehicle; but the restless animal would not permit him to do so, and he was compelled to hold on the reins to keep him from running away. Jed was angry and excited. More of his attention was devoted to the steamer than to the colt, while the latter needed all his thought and all his skill. He was more intent upon securing the crazy man than the crazy horse.

"Can't you tell the steamboat to stop, cap'n?" said Jed to me, as his horse still reared and plunged.

"I can tell it to stop, but I don't believe it will do so."

"That crazy man will tear somebody to pieces."

"Your colt will tear you to pieces, if you don't look out for him," I replied.

I was no seer, but my words were more prophetic

than I anticipated. Suddenly, in spite of bit and rein, the colt whirled round, and attempted to run up the long pier, which had been extended to deep water. The pier was not wide enough for the wagon to turn from the point where it had stood, and the instant the fractious colt saw the yawning abyss of waters, towards which he was headed, he sheered violently. The forward wheel cut against the body, overturned it, and with a thrill of horror I saw Jed whirled into the lake.

Several men sprang forward to seize the bridle of the furious beast; but the wagon went over into the lake. This time the snipe-bill, which had evidently been keyed into the axletree after the last disaster, did not draw out, as before. The whole vehicle hung together like "the wonderful one-horse shay." For an instant the colt struggled to escape from the weight of the wagon, which was pulling him down, but it was only for an instant; then horse and vehicle dropped into the lake together.

The momentum of the whirl which had tossed Jed into the water carried him a little beyond the place where his team fell, or he might have been entan-

gled in the wreck, and, perhaps, have been kicked to death by the struggles of the infuriate horse. I held my breath with terror and anxiety. for the fate of man and horse. Others shouted and screamed; but for a moment no one did anything to save the animal or his driver. Perceiving a skiff hauled up on the beach, near the upper end of the wharf, I rushed for it with all the speed my half-paralyzed limbs would permit. I pushed it off, and sculled towards Jed, who was floundering in the water, out of his depth, and apparently unable to swim.

I soon reached him, and he had nearly upset the boat in his efforts to get into it, when I begged him to desist, or he would certainly be drowned; but there was no more sense in him than there was in the colt. Cool as he had before been on the land, he was beside himself in the water. As it was impossible for him to get into the frail skiff, he was soon weary of his exertions. I was of mine in keeping him from upsetting the boat. I finally persuaded him to hold on at the stern, till I paddled ashore.

Jed was safe, but the horse was not. He was so entangled in the harness that he could not swim, and his violent efforts soon disabled him. By this time three boats were near enough to do something; but the colt had somehow turned himself over. His head seemed to be caught under water, and he was still at last. A rope was thrown beneath him; but when he was pulled up by the men on the wharf, it was all over with him. The colt was drowned.

Jed was overwhelmed by the disaster. He swore like a pirate; and then people did not seem to pity him. Some of them told him it was his own fault, because he had foolishly driven an unbroken colt upon the pier.

"That colt was worth two hundred dollars of any man's money," muttered he, after he had become a little cooler. "Who's going to pay for him?" he demanded, turning to me.

"I'm not," I replied.

"But I guess that Toppleton boy's folks will have to do it."

"I think not," I replied, in a low tone. "If Tommy's folks don't send you to the state prison, you can't afford to bring in any bills against them."

"What do you mean?" he asked, a little disturbed.

I told him what he had done to Tommy, and that his victim was on board of the Ucayga. He seemed to be alarmed, and wanted to talk with me. I explained the case to him as I understood it, and assured him he would be lucky if he escaped with only the loss of the colt.

"But what do they want of the crazy man?" he continued.

"Christy Holgate?"

"You know all about him, then?"

"I do; he is now one of the engineers on board of that boat."

This information was enough to complete the sum total of Jed's misery. He felt like a planter who had lost his best slave,—for such the penitent had been to his relatives. Then I added that Christy had given up the money; and Jed seemed to feel as though he and his father had been abused. I suggested that it would be fair for them to pay back the money they had received for the penitent's board, as he had earned double the amount for his persecutors.

I left him to find the battalion. He was obliged to hire a horse to take him home. If Tommy Toppleton had been deservedly punished, the Trottwoods had not gained anything, either by their treatment of Christy or by taking the law into their own hands.

CHAPTER XXV.

LET US HAVE PEACE.

THE battalion was encamped in a field on the outskirts of the village. During my absence the evening before, Major Briscoe had drilled the companies, and put them through all their evolutions, to the intense admiration of the Priamites. I learned that our fellows had been treated with great kindness and hospitality by the people, and a portion of the officers had spent the evening with some of " the first families."

When I reached the camp, the battalion was preparing for the march. As soon as I appeared, the officers gathered around me, and wanted to know what had become of Tommy. I found myself placed in a difficult position after the instructions the sufferer had given me. I simply told them we had found Tommy; that he was sick, and had just taken the steamer for home. They asked me a great many questions which I did not answer. I succeeded in turning their attention from Tommy to Christy Holgate, whose narrative I related in part, so as to enable my companions to understand the character of the Trottwoods.

They listened with excited attention when I told them of the fate of Jed's colt; and if they were sorry for the animal, I do not think they sympathized very deeply with the owner in the loss he had incurred. Having told all I had to say, I was anxious to learn the condition of the battalion, and whether there was likely to be a mutiny against the new order of things.

"Barnscott and two or three others are a little grouty, but every officer and man does his duty faithfully," replied Briscoe, in answer to my questions. "I don't think we shall have any trouble."

"I hope not."

"I never saw the fellows drill so well as they did last night," added the major. "The crowd that looked on frequently applauded them. The dress parade was absolutely perfect."

"Then you expect to win the banner on Friday."

" Of course I do," laughed Briscoe.

"They say the Wimpleton Battalion has been increasing in numbers lately. There are over two hundred students on the other side of the lake, and they turn out three companies."

"Their numbers won't help them in a drill. On the contrary, they have so many new recruits that our chances are improved."

"But the drill comes off to-morrow, Major Briscoe. Of course you don't expect to march round to Centreport now."

"No; certainly not; but I intend to go to Hitaca to-day. We shall take it easy, and arrive by five o'clock this afternoon. We can show off a little there to-night, and take the steamer in the morning down the lake. We will land at Gulfport, and march the rest of the way. This was what we agreed upon last night."

"I don't think we can do any better," I replied. "Tommy told me he wished you to use his pony. You are a field officer, and are entitled to be mounted."

"I am very much obliged to him, though I can't help thinking the message is a very strange one to come from him to me."

"I don't think so. Tommy has switched off."

"Switched off?"

"Precisely so. That's a railroad phrase, and means that he has turned over a new leaf. Tommy did not say much, but he accepts the situation, and means to make the best of it."

"I hope it is true."

"I think it is, but time alone can prove it. I am afraid he is going to be sick."

"I should think he would be, if he has switched off. It will be a great change of diet for him."

"Tommy was never a bad fellow. If you could only get the conceit out of him, he would be a good fellow. Being the biggest toad in the puddle did not agree with his constitution."

"Well, I don't know but that is enough to spoil almost any fellow. Did Jed thrash him, or anything of that sort," inquired the major, curiously.

"I promised Tommy that I would not say anything about it. Don't ask me, Briscoe."

"I won't."

"He feels very sore."

"In his bones?"

"In spirit; and in his bones, too. I think he must have taken a severe cold, for I cannot account for his condition in any other way."

The battalion had formed in column, and the march to Hitaca was commenced. It was a magnificent day, and our fellows had rested enough to make them fresh and vigorous. The band played its choicest airs, and I never saw soldiers march better than those of the battalion. The applause bestowed upon them by the Priamites stimulated them to do their best. We were followed for some distance by the juvenile portion of the people of the town, but they soon left us; the "route step" was ordered, and we went along as happily as though we had not just passed through the "war of the students."

The scenery in this locality was magnificent. There are half a dozen cataracts in the vicinity of Hitaca, one of which is fifty feet higher than Niagara, though, of course, its volume of water is vastly less. Our march, therefore, was full of interest, and, with the sublime and beautiful around us, we knew no such thing as fatigue. Halting for an hour for dinner, we entered Hitaca in the middle of the afternoon, almost as fresh as when we started, for we had made frequent stops to rest and view the scenery.

We were handsomely received by some of the principal citizens, who had been apprised of our approach. A field, near the head of the lake, was appropriated to our reception, and we were invited to a collation in the evening. We pitched our tents, brushed the dust from our uniforms, and soon looked as spruce and tidy as when we started.

"We shall be full of soldiers to-night," said one of the gentlemen who visited us to me.

"We are only a hundred and fifty," I replied.

"But the others will be here to-night."

"What others, sir?" I inquired.

"Why, the battalion from the other side of the lake — the Wimpleton students," laughed the gentleman, as though he were familiar with the quarrel which had so long existed between the two institutions.

"Indeed! Are they coming too?" I exclaimed,

astonished at the information; though I need not have been, for one side never did anything in which the other did not immediately follow suit.

"We heard of them at Port Gunga this morning, and they must be here very soon," answered the citizen.

I did not exactly like the idea of meeting the Wimpletonians at first. I dreaded a collision of any kind, which the rivalry between the two Institutes was likely to produce. I went to Major Briscoe at once with the information.

"Good!" replied he. "I am glad we arrived first."

"We must keep our men close to-night, or there may be a row, which would be very mortifying to all of us."

"We will not have any row, or anything of the kind. Colonel Wimpleton and Major Toppleton may quarrel, if they are so minded, but I will have nothing to do with their feud. We will do the handsome thing, Skotchley."

"What's that?" I asked, with deep interest.

"Let us have peace," said the major, impressively; and I am not sure he was not the original author of this celebrated expression. "It takes two to quarrel. We will be the first to hold out the olive-branch. I purpose to march out and escort the Wimpletonians into town with all the honors. We will treat them with the utmost respect and consideration; and I am sure there will be nothing but the best of feeling."

"I like that," I replied, with emphasis.

"If we are cross and sullen, they will also be so; and then it won't take much to get up a quarrel."

I was delighted with this proposition. It was exactly in accordance with my own feelings. Major Briscoe ordered the lines to be formed, and then resolved the battalion into a hollow square. He stated briefly that the Wimpletonians were on the march for Hitaca, and would soon arrive. He was in favor of conciliation and good feeling, especially as we were to drill with them the next day. He meant to be courteous to them, and should, therefore, tender them an escort. The fellows clapped their hands, perhaps with a few exceptions. Briscoe then cautioned his officers and men to treat our rivals as though they were our best friends.

The speech concluded, the battalion broke into column, and we marched out on the Southport road. We halted just outside of the town, and Briscoe appointed me to go forward and meet the Wimpletonians. I was to "do the pleasant" in the most agreeable manner, to tender the escort, and arrange the formalities according to the instructions given me by the major. I walked about half a mile, and stopped to view a beautiful cascade. While I was appreciating its beauties, I heard the drum-beat of the Wimpleton column. I waited until it came up.

Magnanimous as I was disposed to be on my errand of peace, I could not help feeling that our rivals did not quite come up to our standard. Their uniforms were not so new and bright, and they had only a drum corps. I stepped up to Major Ben Pinkerton, who was in command, and, saluting him with my sword, delivered my message.

"That's handsome, and I'm very much obliged to you," replied the major. "I'll speak to our fellows, and give you an answer in a few moments."

He halted his column, and, after consulting his officers and men, informed me that the polite offer

18

of Major Briscoe was gratefully accepted. I had delicacy enough to retire, after I had stated the programme suggested by my commander, in order to enable Major Pinkerton to give such instructions to his force as the unexpected meeting might require. I did not hear what he said to them, but I have no doubt they were substantially the same as those to which I had listened in our own battalion.

The march was resumed, and in due time, the Wimpletonians reached our battalion, which was drawn up in line at the side of the road.

"Present — arms!" shouted Major Briscoe; and the band played the appropriate air.

The Centreport battalion marched by the other, and, in turn, forming at the side of the road, presented arms, while we marched in front of it. We then took the head of the column, and escorted our guests into Hitaca, where we were received with applause. On the ground appropriated to the Wimpletonians we presented arms again. The two majors met, shook hands, and appeared to be the best of friends. In fact it was a jolly time. We helped the Wimps pitch their tents, and did all we could to assist them. Such a fraternizing of ancient enemies was never seen, and I began to think we should get to hugging one another before the scene was finished.

At seven o'clock we formed again. More courtesies followed. The majors each reviewed the battalion of the other, and we marched in one column to the festivities of the evening. We had a grand time,— all the better for the sudden and unexpected meeting with the Wimpletonians. At ten we went to our camps.

CHAPTER XXVI.

TOPPLETON TRIUMPHANT.

AT an early hour the next morning, Briscoe called me, and the battalion was soon on its feet. At half past five we had finished breakfast, and everything was ready to embark in the steamer. Not a little to our surprise, we saw that the Wimpletonians, who were encamped near us, were under arms. Knowing that we were to leave before them, they tendered us an escort, which was gratefully accepted. We marched down to the landing-place, countermarched, presented arms, and saluted, each battalion in its turn. When we were on the promenade deck of the boat, we cheered each other with abundant good will. So far as the relations of the two Institutes were concerned, the millennium appeared to have come; for, instead of battling with each other on the slopes of the Horse Shoe, as we had done during the preceding season, we were trying to see which could outdo the other in courtesy and good feeling.

As the Ucayga did not start till three quarters of an hour later, Wolf Penniman came on board of the steamer to see us. No one could have been more delighted than he was when he saw the rival academies on such friendly terms. He declared that it did his heart good to see the sight, and that he should almost be willing to die if he could only see Colonel Wimpleton and Major Toppleton reconciled to each other.

"I have some hopes of it," he added, "after what I have seen to-day and last evening."

"I don't know," I replied, doubtfully. "They have been quarrelling for several years, and it will be hard for them to make up."

"To brake up, you mean," added Wolf, in railroad parlance.

"Since Waddie and Tommy have both switched off, it is possible that their fathers may brake up. But how was Tommy when you left him?"

"He was quite sick. I sat with him most of the

time, in my state-room, during the passage, and I was satisfied that he had indeed switched off. He confessed to me that he had been rather rough on the fellows. When the boat arrived at Centreport, he concluded to go down to Ucayga with me, and return so that I could see him home at noon. I think the events of the last few days have knocked the conceit all out of him. He is particularly grateful to you, Ned, for what you did, after he had treated you so shabbily. That's what turns an enemy into a friend."

"I was trying to imitate your example, Wolf, for I believe in it."

"O, my example is nothing! So far as Waddie was concerned, I only did what my mother taught me — 'Love your enemies.' That's the true principle. It is hard sometimes, but it pays in the long run, or the short one either. I only hope that Tommy will do as well as Waddie has done. After we had landed our passengers at Centreport, I ran the Ucayga over to Middleport, and, procuring a carriage, conveyed Tommy to his father's house. The family were very much alarmed about him, and sent for the physician.

I shouldn't wonder if he had a fever. I staid with him till it was time for the boat to make her afternoon trip."

"Did you see Grace?" I asked.

"I did," replied Wolf, blushing. "She was very grateful to us for what we had done for her brother. I shall see him again to-day noon."

The bell rang for the departure of the boat, and Wolf hurried on shore. As the old steamer worked out from the wharf, the Wimpletonians cheered us again, and we lustily returned their parting salute. I saw Waddie in the ranks, as I had seen him several times before. He did his duty as a private, and I was told that he never even suggested any orders, much less dictated the movements of the battalion. When he was consulted, he gave his opinion freely; but he never put himself forward, and positively refused to accept any office.

Our battalion formed almost the entire company of passengers on the railroad boat. The fight between the two lines did not rage very fiercely after the first season. Major Toppleton always said he intended to do something to recover his lost ground, but he had accomplished nothing yet. He had caused a partial survey to be made for a continuation of the Lake Shore Railroad to Hitaca, but the expense of constructing the road through the wild region was too appalling even for him.

Colonel Wimpleton was waiting to see what the major intended to do. When he found that the Ucayga, working according to the plan arranged by Wolf, took the greater portion of the travel, he concluded not to build another steamer at present. The steamboat line was paying well, and another boat might carry the balance over to the other side of the ledger.

On the other hand, the Lake Shore Railroad was doing a good business with its local freight and passengers, so that the major hesitated before he embarked on a new venture. The first excitement of the competition had subsided, and I am sorry to add, that the personal habits of Colonel Wimpleton were such that he did not give much attention to business of any kind.

Our battalion landed at Gulfport, and immediately marched for Centreport, where the prize drill was to take place. At the picnic grounds we halted for rest and drill. The companies were addressed by the major and by the captains, in order to fire their zeal in the approaching friendly contest with the Wimpletonians. Our fellows drilled splendidly, and I was morally certain that we should carry off the banner. The march was resumed, and when we arrived at the entrance of the town, we were met by the Wimpletonians, who had come down from Hitaca in the Ucayga. All the courtesies we had practised before were gone through with again; and under their escort we marched to the green in front of the Wimpleton Institute, where the drill was to take place.

Already a great crowd of people from both sides of the lake had assembled to witness the show. The two battalions were dismissed for half an hour, and our new-made friends invited us to the refectory of the Institute, where a substantial collation had been provided for the contestants. The rival students mingled together in harmony, and the utmost good will prevailed. Parties on both sides declared that whatever the result of the contest, they should be satisfied; and there were not wanting those on each side who hoped that the other would win the prize.

Colonel Wimpleton was present, but Major Topple-ton was detained at home by the illness of Tommy. The judges were West Pointers, having no interest in either party, and we all expected a just judgment from them. At one o'clock we formed in line, and both battalions were reviewed by Colonel Wimpleton and the judges. Then each company alternately, one from the Centreport battalion, and then one from the Middleport, was drilled separately. The Wimpletoni-ans followed with their battalion movements, and the contest was concluded by the Toppletonians.

There were three judges, each of whom estimated the excellence of each company and each battalion on a scale of one hundred. The average of their figures, made without consultation among themselves, was taken as the mark of the company or battalion. As the Wimpleton battalion had three companies, while the other had but two, two thirds of the total of its marks were taken as its aggregate for the company drill. The results of the company and the battalion drill of each party were then added together, and the one which had the most was entitled to the banner.

The chairman of the judges, after a hollow square

of both battalions had been formed, stepped forward
to announce the decision. He began by commending
both parties for the friendly spirit they had exhibited.
He then praised the general excellence of the drill in
both battalions, declaring that it would compare very
favorably with that of any volunteer organization
which the speaker had ever witnessed. Both sides
lustily applauded this statement, and when the noise
had subsided, the chairman proceeded to read the
figures of the several judges. The Toppleton battalion was ninety-three, while the Wimpleton was eighty-
four; and Company A of the former had the highest
mark for company drill. These results decided the
contest in our favor, and the banner was awarded to
Toppleton by a majority of twenty-two marks.

The Wimpletonians applauded with all their might.
When the result had been read, I saw Colonel Wimpleton biting his lips; but if he was disposed to indulge in any unpleasant remarks, the generous conduct
of the battalion which bore his name silenced him.
It was a fair thing all around; but it ought to be said,
in justice to the Wimpletonians, that they had many
new recruits, whose clumsiness affected the general
result.

Our fellows were more than satisfied: they had won the prize; but what was better, they had **won** the hearts of their rivals. The beginning of all this friendly feeling was the act of Briscoe in tendering the escort to the Wimpletonians. A sneer, a few hard words, or even a little coldness on our part, would have kept alive and fanned the old feeling of resentment. We had not been able to beat our rivals on the hard-fought field of the Horse Shoe, but we had conquered them with the mighty weapon of love, and our victory was complete. "Love your enemies," Wolf would have said, if he had been there; and the blessed truth is as good for boys' play as it is for the serious business of life.

The Wimpletonians invited us to spend the afternoon with them, and we did so. Towards night we were ferried across the lake by our friends, and everything was "lovely" to the end. As soon as our battalion landed, I hastened to the house of Major Toppleton, to see Tommy. He was really very sick; but he was glad to see me, and I told him all that had transpired since he left us. He was very sorry for the loss of Jed's colt; but he smiled with genuine satisfaction when I told him how we had made friends of the Wimpletonians.

I could not believe he was the same arrogant, conceited, tyrannical Tommy Toppleton I had known so long; but he was sick, and there was no assurance that he would not have a moral relapse when his physical health was restored. For a fortnight he did not go out of his chamber. Every day, at noon, Wolf came over to see him — and Grace. Then he began to improve, and in a short time went out. Then Wolf told him about Waddie, and the vast change which had been wrought in him; how everybody on the other side loved him, and would do anything for him; and how Ben Pinkerton had insisted upon resigning, in order that Waddie might be again elected major of the battalion.

Tommy listened to the story with deep interest. He did not say anything. He made no promises, as his rival and prototype on the other side had done; but as the months rolled on, we realized that he was another fellow. He imitated the example of Waddie, and took his place as a private in one of the companies. I shall never forget the love and devotion which his mother and Grace always manifested towards him, for he was another boy in the house as well as abroad. His father was more reserved, and said nothing; but he could not help being impressed by the altered behavior of his son.

If Colonel Wimpleton and Major Toppleton still kept up their former ill will and resentment, it was confined to them, for the two Institutes could no longer be regarded as the rival academies. Each visited the other occasionally, and at one of these meetings some one proposed that the two battalions should be consolidated into a regiment. Tommy and Waddie, who had cordially joined hands, favored the proposition. It was carefully discussed for a whole afternoon, and a committee appointed to arrange the union. The two battalions agreed to meet the next holiday on the Horse Shoe to hear the report.

When the day came, it proved to be an exceedingly interesting occasion. The committee reported that each battalion should retain its present organization for separate parades. Field and staff officers were to be elected or appointed for joint parades. A colonel and lieutenant colonel were to be elected. Pinkerton was to be major, and Briscoe adjutant. A ballot for the two field officers to be elected resulted in the choice of Tommy Toppleton as colonel, and Waddie Wimpleton as lieutenant colonel, for they were really the two most popular fellows in the regiment, under the new order of things. Both of them, with the modesty becoming the new life upon which they had entered, declined, and insisted that Pinkerton and Briscoe should have the highest positions; but we finally persuaded them to accept, and we were never sorry for their action or our own.

In the fall, the regiment marched entirely around the lake, using a fortnight for the tour, and had a magnificent time. We did not stop at Trottwood's this time, though we saw Jed and his father at work in the field. They never troubled Christy Holgate, and I doubt whether he ever went near them. Peace and harmony reigned throughout the regiment. We camped one night on High Bluff, and laughed over the war of the students which had been fought there; but I think all of us were satisfied with the final result, when Tommy Toppleton switched off.

Christy Holgate was not disturbed by the officers

of justice. He was a temperate, well-behaved man, and no one was disposed to meddle with him after he had made all the reparation in his power for his crime. Mr. Penniman divided the labor on the boat with him, so that Christy ran the Ucayga from Centreport to Hitaca, and down to the same point the next morning. This arrangement enabled the Pennimans to occupy their place in Middleport, though Wolf was absent much of the time. Christy moved his family to Hitaca, so that he was with them every night.

But I have told my part of the story, and if the moral of it is not already apparent, I will simply add, that, when you find yourself leading a wicked or useless life, — in other words, when you are on the wrong track, — do as my good friend Tommy Toppleton did — SWITCH OFF.